CASE OF THE

RAGIN'
CAJUN
BOOK 13

J.M. POOLE

Secret Staircase Books

I

Case of the Ragin' Cajun
Published by Secret Staircase Books, an imprint of
Columbine Publishing Group, LLC
PO Box 416, Angel Fire, NM 87710

Book layout and design by Secret Staircase Books
Cover image © Felipe de Barros

First trade paperback edition: July, 2021
First e-book edition: July, 2021

* * *

Publisher's Cataloging-in-Publication Data

Poole, J.M.
Case of the Ragin' Cajun / by J.M. Poole.
p. cm.
ISBN 978-1649140562 (paperback)
ISBN 978-1649140579 (e-book)

1. Zachary Anderson (Fictitious character)--Fiction. 2.
New Orleans, Louisiana—Fiction. 3. Amateur sleuth—Fiction.
4. Pet detectives—Fiction. I. Title

Corgi Case Files Mystery Series : Book 13.
Poole, J.M., Corgi Case Files mysteries.

BISAC : FICTION / Mystery & Detective.

813/.54

CONTENTS

Case of the

Ragin' Cajun

J.M. Poole

**Sign up for Jeffrey's newsletter to
get all the latest corgi news—
Click here** AuthorJMPoole.com

ACKNOWLEDGMENTS

I'm often asked whether I have ever attended any book signings. The answer to that is a resounding *no*. Like Zack, I view them as a popularity contest, and I've seen my fair share of authors sitting (forlornly) on the other side of the table, waiting eagerly for someone to look their way. As for this book, I had originally plotted out a Mississippi river cruise, culminating in an arrival to the Big Easy, but as you could probably deduce, the dogs wouldn't be allowed on a boat. Not unless I tried to pass them off as service dogs, and I figure if I ever did that, I'd be doing a disservice to real service dogs everywhere. So, I thought about how much I don't like public speaking, and voila! The story was plotted in no time flat.

Helping me out with the creation of this book, as always, is my lovely wife, Giliane. I pass ideas by her all the time, and most of the time, she likes them. Also on the list are some beta readers. Jason, Carol, Caryl, Diane, Louise, Michelle, and Hellen. I appreciate you guys taking the time to help me out and keep me looking as good as possible!

Also high on that list are Secret Staircase Books' set of beta readers: Marcia, Susan, Sandra, Judith, and Paula. You guys are also part of my team, and you are all very much appreciated!

With all that being said, I'd like to thank you, the reader, for choosing my book from all the hundreds of thousands out there to choose from! You guys rock!

For Giliane —

*We're going to get you to Pomme Valley
yet! Fingers crossed!*

ONE

"Zachary, have you ever been to New Orleans? I have, a few times. You have no idea how much history this town has."

"Yep," I confirmed, "I've been here before. Sadly, I have to admit that I didn't really get a chance to look around, and I've regretted it ever since. I've always wanted to walk along Bourbon Street, check out the shops, and try some of the food this area is known for. I know it's the tourist-y thing to do, but I don't care. I've always loved the look and *feel* of this place."

"Well, we're here now. You're finally going to get your chance. What about you two? Vance? Tori? Have you ever been to New Orleans?"

Before I go any further, I suppose I should give you some context. First off, my name is Zachary Anderson, but everyone calls me Zack. That is, everyone but my fiancée, Jillian Cooper, who always seems to call me Zachary. As if you couldn't

tell, she's here with me. We are both from a little town in southwestern Oregon called Pomme
Valley. Our town is less than ten miles southwest
from Medford, and about thirty minutes east of
Grants Pass. PV, as we like to call it, is known for
its peaceful living, quiet atmosphere, and being a
crime-free town.

Kinda.

As my friend Vance eagerly reminds me, ever
since I moved to town, the crime of the big city
seemingly moved with me. We've had multiple
murders, brazen thefts, and even had a span of
time where innocent dogs were stolen. And, as if to
prove my friend's point, the last time Jillian and I
went on vacation, we managed to find a dead body
and get dragged into the local police investigation.

But, I'd like to say that, if not for Sherlock and
Watson, I never would have known anything was
happening, let alone be paid to help solve crimes.
Now, I know some of you are probably shaking
your head, wondering how two fictitious characters could possibly help solve real crimes. Well, in
my case, Sherlock and Watson are real, only they
aren't humans.

They are dogs.

I adopted Sherlock practically the moment I
first set foot in Pomme Valley. My best friend from
high school just happened to live in PV as well, and
not only was he still a prankster at heart, Harrison
Watt was the town veterinarian. His office handled all rescue dogs, too, which meant that he was

always on the lookout for someone to adopt one of his dogs. Well, Harry played his cards right, had the timing down perfectly, and just like that, I suddenly had something in common with the queen of England: we both owned a corgi.

Sherlock is a tri-colored bundle of energy. It wasn't until I researched the breed online that I learned that this particular dog was a member of the herding group, and that meant this dog was very active. Thankfully, all my misgivings were gone after the first night of ownership. Having been recently widowed just a few months before becoming a resident of Oregon, it turned out owning a dog was just what I needed. That's about the time Harry brought me a second corgi. This one was a red and white female, who I named Watson, much to the horror of my friends. They all figured naming a little girl like that was going to emotionally scar her for life. But, I stuck to my guns and just like that, I became the proud daddy of two little corgis. Now, several years later, I can honestly say that I don't even remember what life was like without a dog, nor would I ever want to again.

Now, I should give you a little background about myself. I'm a romance writer, and I should inform you that I sell an obscene amount of books each month. So many that it affords me a very comfortable lifestyle. I'm also the owner of my own private winery. Lentari Cellars had been started by the late Bonnie Davies, a distant relative of my deceased wife, Samantha. After Bonnie passed, which wasn't that long after my own wife, I received a life-changing letter, telling me that Samantha and I had inherited great-aunt Bonnie's estate, and that included the winery.

You had better believe I made some enemies that day. There are those, who won't be named, who feel that I had no business accepting something which should have stayed with the family. Well, I'm not that easily intimidated, so the winery was going to stay with me. I re-opened at the earliest opportunity.

Nowadays, the winery pulls in almost as much as my book sales. Since I am not a fan of wine, and know next-to-nothing about how to make it, I was more than happy to allow Lentari Cellar's former master vintner, Caden Burne, to resume his duties, giving Caden full control over Lentari Cellars' day-to-day operation. All I have to do is sign the checks.

And finally, if all that wasn't enough, as I previously mentioned, I'm a paid consultant for the local police force. But, in my defense, the local PD isn't really concerned with my powers of deductive reasoning. That all falls on my two dogs. Sherlock and Watson, true to their namesakes, can solve crimes better than any human detective, and that includes my good friend Vance Samuelson, who just so happens to be a detective on the police force. Whenever he's working a case, and needs the help of their Royal Canineships, he gives me a buzz and I'll take the dogs wherever they need to go. I've also since learned to pay *close* attention to my canine companions whenever we're working a case. Whatever catches the dogs' attention will have me reaching for my phone to take a picture. Then, after enough pictures, or corgi clues as I have started calling them, have been collected, Jillian and I will have a good laugh as we review them and try to piece together what all the pictures mean. Oftentimes, I'll enlist the help of the gang, since every Friday night we get together for dinner and share what experiences we've all had the past week.

To this date, none of us have been able to solve a case faster than the dogs. It's a bitter point of contention with Vance, and I have secretly vowed to figure out one of these cases before they do. When it happens, expect the fireworks.

Fast forward to the present day. The four of us, namely myself, Jillian, Vance, and Tori, were speeding along in a cab, on our way to a convention center in New Orleans, Louisiana. Also with us were the dogs, who at the moment, were sitting on each of our laps so they could look out the windows. Yes, we were getting dog hair all over us, but we came prepared: there were several lint rollers in my backpack.

"I still can't believe this is happening," Tori was saying.

Tori is Vance's wife. She's tall, has red hair, green eyes, and is third-generation Irish. She and Vance have been married for fifteen years now, which was pretty much the reason why we were on this excursion.

Let me explain.

Late last year, I was approached by Vance, who asked me if I would be willing to write Tori into one of my books, using her likeness, personality, quirks, etc. He wanted to surprise her for their fifteenth anniversary. Well, I did one better. I came up with a story based on a strong, independent woman living in the middle of Ireland during the Great Potato Famine, which occurred in the mid-19th century. My female protagonist has to endure some pretty dire circumstances in order to keep her family fed and protected. *Heart of Éire* was born that day. I remember sitting there with Vance, at Casa de Joe's, and sketching out a rough plot. It actually shocked me how fast I came up with the story. Then again, Ireland has always been one of my favorite countries to visit, and as such, it wasn't particularly hard for me to come up with a story based on the Emerald Isle.

No mere ties connect this one, though. *Heart of Éire* takes place in Ireland, is all about Ireland, and should appeal to anyone who has Irish blood in them. Well, little did I know how badly I had misjudged that. For the first time ever, thanks to the sales of this book, I hit the *New York Times* Best Sellers List, surprising everyone, including my publisher.

And *that* was why we were here. My publisher talked me into attending a book signing, which if you're familiar with my history, you will know is an absolute rarity. I've never cared for signings. Why? Well, have you ever seen any? The last few I've witnessed were so sad that they bordered on pathetic. The last author I saw, for example, was sitting behind a rectangular table in the middle of a bookstore. Stacks of his books were on either side of him and there he was, hands clasped in front of him, pen at the ready, as he waited for someone to make eye contact with him. He wasn't talking, he wasn't smiling, but instead, just waiting for an opportunity to shove his book in front of someone's face.

That wasn't for me. So, if I was going to be talked into doing one of these things, then it was going to be on *my* terms. At no point would it be required for me to sit behind one of these tables, unless I chose to do so. I would be up, moving around, and interacting with anyone who chose to stop. Additionally, I would not be alone. I would have a few friends to talk with, since—in my opinion—most people would be willing to approach an author if he/she appears friendly and not standoffish.

I'd like to say that was why Vance and Tori were with us, but to be honest, they were here because … well, let's face it. *They* were the reason *Heart of Éire* was written. I was splitting the proceeds from this particular book with them, fifty-fifty, and after the Samuelsons had seen the size of the first (of many) royalty check with their names on it, they had readily accepted my invitation to join me and Jillian in New Orleans. All expenses paid, of course. This time, though, I wasn't the one picking up the tab, nor was Jillian. It was one of my stipulations for my publisher. I honestly thought it was my ace in the hole for getting them to drop this ridiculous request of theirs. Much to my surprise, they agreed. They even agreed to my request of bringing along the dogs, even going so far as making them purchase two extra tickets so they could ride in the plane's cabin with us. I guess I shouldn't be too surprised. After all, I make them a ton of money.

"Here we are," the driver announced, as he pulled the van into the unloading zone in front of the biggest convention center I have ever seen. "I hope you all have fun in there!"

I slipped a few bills into the driver's tip jar, thanked him, and followed the rest of my group outside. Jillian handed me Sherlock's leash while she held onto Watson's. I waited to see if anyone was going to take the lead when I noticed that the others had fallen back and were currently standing behind me. Everyone's eyes were on me.

"I guess this is my show. Fine. I'm supposed to be meeting someone from MCU somewhere in there, so might as well start looking. Come on, guys. We're heading inside."

As I gave a gentle tug on the leash, Sherlock turned to look back at me, gave himself a solid shake, and then headed toward a long row of glass doors—all propped open—which led inside. Behind me, I could hear the girls talking.

"I'm so surprised that we're doing this," Jillian was saying.

"Why?" Tori wanted to know.

"Zachary absolutely *hates* book signings. He views them as popularity contests, and it's something he's steadfastly against. Then again, I think he was tired of looking at bridal venues with me."

"Oh? You two can't decide where to get married?" Tori asked.

"His guest list isn't too bad," Jillian confirmed, "but mine? It's pure insanity. I know everyone in PV, and if I leave someone off the guest list, then feelings will be hurt. We have to be sure to invite everyone."

"That's a lot of people," Tori agreed.

"Right? I've made a few calls, but it doesn't look good. I think we might have to have the wedding outside of PV."

"I'll keep my eyes and ears open for you, too," Tori promised.

"Thank you. Did Vance say anything about Zack's reluctance to do this signing?"

"A little. He's an author, and a very successful one. Does he really hate book signings that much?"

"He does," Jillian confirmed.

"Then, why did he agree to do it?" I heard Tori softly ask.

"I would imagine it's because of you and Vance," Jillian guessed. "He told me he may have written this book, but he owes its creation to you. Or, more specifically, Vance."

"Hmm?" Vance asked, overhearing his name.

"Oh, it's nothing," Tori assured him. "We're just chatting."

"About?"

"How much you owe Zack," Tori giggled.

I grinned to myself and elected to remain quiet.

"Have any of your titles ever sold this well before?" Vance asked me a few minutes later, in a low voice, once the girls had returned to their conversation.

"No," I said, as I reached the front doors and stepped aside to let the girls go through first. Vance quickly mimicked me. "In order to have a shot at hitting the *New York Times* list, you have to sell a minimum of 5,000 copies in a single week. Many of the books sell more, but that's the barest minimum in order to be considered. I've been trying to hit this particular milestone for quite a while."

"Good grief, buddy," Vance whispered. "How many copies have been sold so far?"

"Honestly? I don't know. But, based on the last three royalty checks, and the fact that each check is bigger than the previous month's, I'd say it's doing pretty darn good."

"I'll say," Vance said, nodding. "I think we've already covered Vick and Tiffany's college education, and there's still plenty left over." My friend looked over at me and held up a fist. "Thanks, pal. I mean it."

I bumped his fist with my own. "Any time,

amigo. Have you figured out what you're going to do yet with your share of the royalties? I just heard you say something to the effect of the girls' college tuitions are paid for. Any other plans?"

"No freakin' idea, pal," Vance admitted. "What about you?"

"Me, personally? I'm seriously considering creating the ultimate man-cave. I'm talking full-size arcade games, pinball machines, and, of course, what arcade would be complete without skee-ball?"

"Skee-ball," Vance moaned, as a look of pure bliss passed across his features. "Oh, man, I had forgotten how much I love that game. What a fantastic idea! You're looking for one now?"

"I'm thinking two, but I want them to be official games, not the cheap reproductions. So, I've been checking with arcades. Someone, somewhere, has gotta be selling some of those original units."

"If you find one, then you let me know, okay?"

Vance and I bumped fists again. "You got it. Holy crap on a cracker! Look who it is!"

Our little group came to an immediate stop and it was all I could do to not start sputtering like an idiot. There, in front of me, was the author of *The Da Vinci Code*.

"It's Dan Brown!" I continued.

Jillian's eyes widened appreciatively, while Vance and Tori politely nodded.

"He wrote the Robert Langdon series," I hastily explained. "*Angels & Demons*, *The Da Vinci Code*,

Lost Symbol, and so on. Wow. I had no idea he was going to be here."

The world-famous author was getting ready to pass me with his entourage when he noticed Sherlock and Watson. He paused long enough to give each of them a pat before turning to me.

"Cute dogs. You should put them in a book."

I felt my mouth open with surprise. Dan Brown was talking to me! "I, er, have considered it, many times. They're more famous than I'll ever be."

Dan Brown laughed heartily and gave me a friendly slap on the shoulder before moving on. Vance immediately sidled up to me and pointed at my shoulder.

"Let me guess. You're never going to wash it again, are you?"

"Bite me, pal."

"How many of these people do you recognize?" Jillian wanted to know, as we slowly made our way deeper into the convention center. Booths and tables were everywhere. "Would anyone know you?"

I shrugged. "Perhaps. Then again, I'm not going to approach every person and ask, either. Oh, man. I just spotted someone else I know."

"Someone you've met or someone you've heard of?"

"Someone I've heard of," I clarified. "His debut novel is in my top five favorite books of all time."

Tori perked up. "Oh? Who is it?"

"Andy Weir. He wrote *The Martian*."

Vance was nodding this time. "Oh, I've seen that movie. It stars Matt Damon, right?"

"Right," I confirmed. I turned back to see if he was still there, but was surprised to see Andy Weir standing directly before me. "Umm, hey there. Sorry. I guess I should've kept my voice down."

A hand was thrust in my direction. "Don't be. You've read my work? What would you say if I told you that I've read yours, too? I know who you are, Mr. McGee."

Jim McGee was the name of my pseudonym for this newest novel.

"Ah, er, um ..."

"Wow, that doesn't happen often," Jillian teased. "You've rendered him speechless!"

Andy Weir's hand clasped my own. "But, I also know you're Zachary Anderson, aren't you?"

"Uh, well, I, er ..."

"Both my wife and I have read *Heart of Éire*. Well done, Mr. Anderson. I've never wanted to visit Ireland more than I do right now. You did a great job."

"Th-thanks. I appreciate that, I really do."

The author of *The Martian* wandered off. Turning to Jillian, I shook my head. My face felt like it was on fire, so I can only imagine it was as red as a Coke can.

"You handled that well," Jillian teased.

"Talk about the mother of all brain farts," I groaned. "I must have sounded like a babbling idiot."

"You were fine, Zachary. And to think he knew

who you were! That must make you feel good."

We walked on, passing by booths with authors sitting quietly behind tables laden with books. We encountered vendors selling electronic reading devices, VR glasses, and just about everything else you could think of. Artists had set up their portfolios, and in case you're wondering why artists were there, it's because every artist's dream was similar to us authors: get their works in the hands of as many people as possible. In an artist's case, if they could convince a popular author to use them to create their covers, well, it would mean a huge boost to the artist's image. I also passed newly christened editors trying to get new clients, and I even found someone who had created some beautiful, hand-stitched leather journals.

"This one looks like dragon scales," Jillian said, as she pointed to a dark green five by eight inch leather journal.

"And this one looks like an ancient manuscript," I observed. I grinned at the young guy, who was looking eagerly at us, hoping to make a sale. "I'll take them both."

We stopped at four other booths before I finally spotted something that drew me up short. "Hmm, I think I might've found the person we're supposed to be meeting."

Standing off to the side, holding up a sign like you've probably seen at the airports where drivers were looking for their fares, was a young woman in her late twenties. I thought she was a little young to be wearing a three-piece suit, but she pulled it off quite well. Glancing down at my own jeans and tee shirt, I cringed. No one had said there would be a dress code here. As I approached, I watched the woman's head swivel in my direction, but before she could say anything, her eyes dropped down to the floor and saw the dogs. Her bored expression was quickly replaced by one of pure delight.

"Corgis! Oh, I so love the breed. They ... wait. They told me Mr. Anderson would be traveling with two corgis. Are you Zachary Anderson?"

I held out a hand. "Call me Zack. Is everyone here dressed as nicely as you are? I'm kinda feelin' like a hick right about now."

The girl seized my hand and pumped it up and down. "Isabella Murphy. Pleased to meet you, Mr. Anderson. Oh, I'm sorry. Zack. And no, don't worry about attire. We're just glad you're here."

The introductions were made, and I'm thankful to have been able to get the dogs included before any glass could be shattered. Sherlock, somehow, always knew when introductions were being made and when he was left out. Apparently, that didn't sit well with the corgi. Once everyone was acquainted, I pointed in the direction everyone seemed to be walking.

"So, is that where we're supposed to go? I have to tell you, Isabella, I haven't been to a book signing in, well, decades. I usually don't do these."

"We know you don't," Isabella said, nodding.

"And call me Bella. It's easier."

"Thanks, Bella. So, who did you tick off in order to get saddled with me for the next couple of days?"

"Once I heard you were coming, I volunteered," Bella told me.

"Are you a fan of Zachary's books?" Jillian asked.

"Every single one of them. And yes, before you ask, Zack, I know about the other pseudonym you use."

"It used to bother me," I confided, "but it doesn't anymore. I'm all right with people knowing. However, I'm pretty sure the sales would take a hit if my primary writing name became known, so I still don't volunteer that information to anyone."

"Which we appreciate," Bella said. She held up an arm and waved us over. "If you'll follow me, I'll show you where we're holding our panel."

I nodded. "Sounds good. I just need to … wait. Hold up, Bella. You guys are conducting a panel? That wasn't part of the arrangement."

Bella stopped and slowly turned around. A sheepish grin was on her face. "They said you were more than likely going to object. So, I've been authorized to … sweeten the pot, if you will."

"What is a *panel*?" Jillian asked.

"It's where there's this big, long table at the front of a large group of people, with microphones, bottles of water, and so on," I explained, still wearing a frown. "The victims, er, *guests*, are then asked questions by a moderator, and sometimes members of the audience. I said to you people I don't like sitting behind a table," I announced, raising my voice.

I know I was starting to sound angry, and I was truly, honestly, sorry about it. However, Jillian had been right. I view these types of gatherings as nothing more than yet another way of showing everyone just how popular you are. Or aren't. Flashbacks to high school, and getting chosen last in practically every sporting event I had ever participated in, came to mind. It was just as much fun then as it was now, which is to say, it *wasn't*.

Isabella was now holding up her hands in a pleading gesture. "Please, Mr. Anderson. Hear me out. If you're willing to participate in the panel, then I've been authorized to offer you and your lovely fiancée your own private table at Antoine's Restaurant tonight, followed by dessert from Café Du Monde."

With a dumbfounded look on her face, Jillian turned to me and excitedly took my arm. "Antoine's? Have you ever been there, Zachary? It's the country's oldest family-run restaurant!"

"Who's Antoine?" Vance wanted to know.

"That restaurant has been around since 1840," I explained. "And, I can tell you they have a wicked Baked Alaska." I looked at Bella, who had a smug smile on her face, as though she knew I was going to agree. "Antoine's is a great place to eat, and I wouldn't mind going back there. However ..."

The smile disappeared from Bella's face.

"... that isn't even close to getting me to agree to join your panel."

"Okay, um, let me see." Bella whipped out her phone and started firing off texts just as fast as she could type them. "Please give me just a moment."

"Who are you talking to?" I wanted to know. "Is it Richard?" I held out a hand and waited for her to pass the phone over. "Let's just cut to the chase, shall we?"

It was my turn to start firing off texts.

"Who's Richard?" I heard Tori ask.

"It's his rep at MCU," Jillian answered. "I've heard the name a few times lately. Even though he isn't Zachary's agent, he acts like it."

"What does MCU stand for?" Vance wanted to know.

"It's an acronym," Jillian said. "Manheim Company Unlimited. However, Zachary came up with a completely different name for them."

Intrigued, Bella sidled closer. "Okay, you've piqued my curiosity. Could I ask you what name he came up with?"

"Man-Chest United."

Bella's eyes widened. "No, he didn't!"

Having overheard the exchange, I handed Bella her phone back. "Believe it. Look at the covers Chastity Wadsworth has released. The vast majority of them have naked man-torsos on them, and the women usually aren't wearing much more. Whether you want to believe it or not, showing a little skin on the covers ends up selling very well."

We then heard a gasp of surprise from Bella. Turning, I could see that she had just read the exchange I had with Richard, and what MCU had just agreed to in order to get my sorry rear up in front of a number of people, doing the one thing I *don't* want to do. Bella turned to look at me and then promptly gave me a mock bow.

"You are the *master*."

Vance couldn't contain his curiosity any further. "What is it? What did he make you guys do?"

"They must truly love you," Bella said. Admiration was written all over her features. "The next time I need to negotiate something, is it okay if I come to you?"

I laughed and nodded. "Lead the way, Bella. I believe your panel is going to be starting shortly, isn't it?"

"Just like that, you've agreed to do this panel thing?" Vance skeptically asked.

"Hey, turns out I do have a price after all. In this case, I just have to do one additional book signing."

"That's not much of an incentive," Tori decided.

"It is if the signing is taking place in London," I added, with a smile.

Jillian clutched my hand tightly in her own. "They're sending you to England for a book signing? My word! Are they covering all of your expenses?"

"They're covering all of *our* expenses," I corrected, as I looked over at our two friends and gave them a thumbs up.

"Hold on," Vance sputtered. "You included us in this? We're getting a free trip to England, too?"

"Yep. We won't be gone too long, maybe three or four days at the most. And, that doesn't include travel days, since it'll take a full day of flying just to get there."

"We're all going?" Jillian exclaimed, delighted.

"I'm just not sure about them," I said, as I looked down at the dogs. "This time around, I think we might need to find a puppy-sitter. I don't know if they'll take them. I'll have to try later."

"That's a very generous offer on MCU's part," Jillian decided.

"I guess I'm more of an introvert than I had thought," I returned. "They know I'm not fond of book signings, and usually they don't press the case like this. Apparently, though, they have discovered my Kryptonite."

Interested, Jillian looked up. "And that would be …?"

I smiled at my fiancée. "*You*, my dear. It wasn't enough to send just me somewhere. MCU now knows I'm more willing to go if *you* are with me."

It was at this time that our group arrived at a set of double doors, both closed. There was a printed paper taped to each door, announcing that the following panels were going to be video recorded and to make certain your cell phones were either set to silent, or else shut off. Eager to comply, I set mine to silent, followed almost immediately by Jillian. Once Vance and Tori had followed suit, Bella gave me an apologetic look and pushed open the two doors.

There was an instant round of applause as nearly a thousand people sprang to their feet and started cheering. Sherlock and Watson, properly spooked, fired off several warning woofs. Watson then hurried to my side and tried to get between my legs. Were all these people cheering because of me? If they were going to continue to do so, then I'd have no choice but to leave, since neither of the dogs would be able to settle down.

Thankfully, Bella came to my rescue. She hurried on to the stage and spoke with a middle-aged woman wearing a red blouse and black slacks. Perhaps she was the moderator of this panel? Whoever she was, she at least had the ability to quiet the crowds. The lady hurriedly grabbed the microphone.

"We have to keep it down, people. You can all see our guest of honor has arrived and is accompanied by his two adorable corgis. We don't want to scare them, do we?"

Bella appeared and guided us over to a cordoned-off area in the front row. But, before I could take a seat, I was guided to a set of stairs leading up to the raised platform. Sighing, I passed Sherlock's leash to Tori and headed for the stairs.

"Welcome, Mr. Anderson!" the woman exclaimed.

I nodded my head, but quickly came to a stop.

Apparently, MCU had let it slip that I had written *Heart of Éire* using my newest pseudonym, namely Jim McGee. What could I say? I needed a name that sounded Irish and it was the first one I thought of. I just don't know how all these people had found out I was the one behind it. I guess I'm not nearly as secretive as I thought.

"I'm Marjorie Sanderson," our host was saying. "I'll be the moderator today for MCU. Do you know the other authors here?"

Other authors? I leaned around Marjorie and saw that three of the chairs were presently occupied: one older man, one younger guy, and a woman who was probably no older than me. And yes, I knew them all. Not personally, mind you, but I've been with my publisher long enough to recognize my fellow MCU authors.

"I did not think they'd be able to get you out here, pal," the younger guy said. "Mark Spears. We met a few years ago, but I don't think you would've remembered."

I didn't, but I wasn't going to let *him* know that.

"Long time, no see, Zack," the older gentleman said, holding out his hand.

Now *him* I knew, having met him three or four times, I think. Jack Dalton has written some fantastic techno-thrillers, featuring heists involving computer hacking, cyber-terrorism, and the like. I took his hand as I got close.

"Good to see you again, Jack."

"Ditto, Anderson. And you owe me twenty

CASE OF THE RAGIN' CAJUN

bucks."

"Huh? I do? For what?"

Jack slapped a twenty onto Mark's outstretched hand. "I bet against you, I'm afraid. I thought for certain there wasn't any way in hell they'd get you up here."

I grinned at Jack and shrugged. "What can I say? Evidently, I *can* be bought."

This was said close enough to a microphone where my comment was picked up and broadcast to everyone present. Laughter and chuckles ensued. The moderator pointed at an empty chair next to the woman's. As I slid into place, I glanced over at her and held out a hand.

"It's been a while, Cassie. It's nice to see you again."

"Oh, my heaven's word," the woman exclaimed. "Mr. Anderson, you remember me?"

Cassie Merryman has been with MCU for a few years. She had a successful cozy mystery series featuring a female barista at a popular coffee house. Cassie's protagonist was single, in her mid-thirties, and sharp as a tack. Her character's keen observational skills caused her to butt heads with the local police department on more than one occasion, which, of course, was where her romantic love interest was employed. Oftentimes, the two of them would work a case together, but typically, Cassie's female sleuth would work her case alone. Oh, I should mention that there were a couple of cats involved, too.

"Of course. My late wife enjoyed your books."

"Your lovely wife has passed away? Oh, I'm so sorry."

"It's not your fault, Cassie. Don't worry about it."

Marjorie stepped up to the microphone and tapped it a few times.

"Okay, I do believe we're ready to get started. And please, for the sake of Mr. Anderson's two adorable dogs, let's keep the chatting and the applause to an absolute minimum. Now, for you newcomers, let's make the introductions."

For the next twenty minutes, I politely sat in my chair, behind this huge white table, and listened while the moderator read the bio for each author and then a list of their popular works. When Marjorie read my name, and then the alias I had written *Heart of Éire* under, the room erupted in applause once again. However, I could also hear both dogs barking.

I ended up waving at the crowd to try and calm them down. Tapping on my microphone a few times, I waited until everyone was quiet.

"Thanks, guys. As you can clearly hear for yourselves, Sherlock and Watson aren't crazy about all this noise."

"Wait a moment," Cassie said, from right beside me. "Your dogs are named Sherlock and Watson?"

"They are, and before you ask, yes, they've solved quite a few crimes. When I'm not writing books, there's a good chance you'll find me helping out the local police department."

"How did I not know that?" the moderator asked, perplexed. "I thought I knew everything about you, Mr. Anderson."

"That isn't something I publicize. Now, let me ask all of you something. Are you all here for *Heart of Éire*?"

There were a number of shouts of affirmation, followed immediately by numerous requests to keep quiet.

"I'm impressed. Thank you all so much for the support. I will go on record to say I typically don't do conventions like this. It's not really my thing. But, now that I'm here, I can answer a few questions, if you like."

"That's a great idea," Marjorie exclaimed. "Let's open the floor for our Q & A session. Does anyone out there have a question for one of our panelists?"

Thankfully, Jack was given the first question. Was there going to be a sequel to his latest novel? Since it clearly sold quite well, the answer to that was a resounding yes.

"This question is for Mr. Anderson."

I looked up to see a young Asian woman holding a wireless microphone and nervously shifting her weight from leg to leg. "Have you ever been to Ireland?"

"I have, yes. Cork, in County Cork, and Dublin. Have you?"

The woman shook her head. "Oh, no, I haven't, but I would love to someday."

"Well, if you do, I would recommend visiting Cork. There's a shop there called Blarney Woollen Mills. They have a fantastic selection of Waterford crystal. Be prepared to drop some bucks if you go. Trust me, you'll love it."

"Next question is for Mr. Anderson."

I looked over at the second podium that had been set up. There was a college-age guy standing there, holding the microphone, and looking as though he was dared to be there.

"So, um, like, you said you've been to Ireland. Have you ever kissed the Blarney Stone?"

A round of laughter erupted.

I shook my head. "No. I can tell you I had every opportunity to, but when it came down to it, no. I wasn't about to be held upside-down and kiss the same area everyone else and their uncle have kissed. Didn't seem very sanitary, if you ask me. Did it give me bad luck? Not that I can tell."

On and on it went. For nearly an hour, my fellow panelists and I answered question after question. Do we ever experience writer's block? How would we go about getting an agent? Is there any value to self-publishing a book?

Finally, near the end of the Q & A session, someone actually asked a decent question, and one that I was surprised hadn't come up until now.

"Mr. Anderson, what was your inspiration for *Heart of Éire*? How did it come to be?"

I leaned forward to rest my elbows on the table. "That is a fantastic question. To best answer it, I think I need to ask a few people to join me up here."

Even though they were at least twenty feet away, I heard Vance groan.

"Come on, guys. Help me persuade my friend Vance and his lovely wife up here. They're the reason *Heart of Éire* was written."

Tori popped up so fast that she resembled a prairie dog poking its head out of its burrow. She hastily pulled Vance to his feet and hurried to the stage.

"Ladies and gents," I began, "can we please welcome Vance and Tori Samuelson, only can we do it softly?"

There was muted laughter.

"You just had to pull me into this, didn't you?" my friend grumbled, as two chairs were hastily placed on my left. "What in the Sam Hill am I doing up here?"

I held my arm out to the crowd and grinned at them. "I think they'd like to hear the story."

"What story?" Vance asked. He refused to look out at the sea of faces staring back at him.

"My pal here," I began, as I slapped a friendly hand on Vance's back, "comes up to me one day and says he'd like to do something special for his and his wife's anniversary. He knew Tori ... say hi, Tori."

"Hello!" Tori all but shouted, waving like she was about ready to board a ride at Disneyland.

"Tori is a fan of my books, so Vance thought it'd be a novel way to ... pardon the pun, by the way… Vance thought it'd be a novel way to appeal to Tori, namely having a character in one of my books based on her. Appearance, personality, etc. I one-upped that and suggested writing a story with her as the main character. Since Tori is Irish, and loves anything to do with Ireland, I set the book in Cork. Vance loved the idea, so right there, sitting on the patio outside in our hometown, we had lunch and I plotted out the events of *Heart of Éire*. And, in case anyone is wondering, I'm sharing the proceeds of the book with him, fifty-fifty. The rest, as they say, is history."

"Mr. Samuelson?" the moderator announced.

Vance sat up straight in his chair. "Yes?"

"You sure are lucky to have such a good, kind, and generous a friend as Mr. Anderson, aren't you?"

"Uh, well … yeah, I guess so."

I held up a hand. "I know some of you are filming this, so to whomever has a copy of that particular video, with that particular observation, could I get you to send me a copy?"

Vance sighed. "Hardy har har, pal."

"Any other questions?" Marjorie asked the audience.

One girl raised her hand. I could see she had to be young, probably in her late teens. She approached the podium, took the microphone from the staff member, and slowly faced me.

"Er, hi, Mr. Anderson. My name is Melody Ashford."

I smiled at the teenager. "Hello there, Melody. What's your question?"

"All right, here's my question. You live in Oregon, don't you?"

I nodded. "I do."

"Have you noticed how often Ireland and Oregon have been mentioned in the news recently?"

Interested, I perked up. "What do you mean, Melody?"

"Take the Irish Crown Jewels. They were missing for over a hundred years, but recently, they were found and returned. The news report also said that the jewels were found in Oregon, but you knew that, didn't you?"

"Believe it or not, I'm aware of it," I said, suppressing a chuckle.

"Rumor has it," the teen continued, "that *you* had something to do with that."

"Imagine that," I said, in a sing-song voice. "And why would you think that?"

"I'm a huge fan of the British royal family. I read everything I can on them, so imagine my surprise when I see a reference to the missing Irish Crown Jewels, and the person who found them is an author who happens to own a couple of corgis ..."

"I happen to know Stephen King has a corgi," I interrupted.

"... named Sherlock or Watson?"

I crossed my arms over my chest. "Ah. That'd be harder to play off, wouldn't it?"

"Was that you, Mr. Anderson? Did you find the

Irish Crown Jewels?"

"That was me," I admitted.

There was a collective gasp from the audience.

"Why didn't you say that from the start?" the teen asked, bewildered. "I would think you'd want everyone to know about that!"

"Because," I answered, "I don't like making a big deal out of it. Yes, I found the jewels and yes, they were returned to their rightful owners."

"Any final questions before we …"

The moderator trailed off as a loud rumbling started. To us, in our cordoned off section of the exposition center, we couldn't see anything, but I can tell you it sure sounded like a pack of elephants was stampeding. Then the shouting began.

"What the blazes is going on?" Vance whispered to me. "Is that supposed to happen at one of these expos?"

"No," I said, growing alarmed. "Marjorie? Do you have any idea what's going on?"

"Stay calm, people," Marjorie ordered. I can only assume our moderator either worked in a prison, or a school at some time because everyone settled down. "Everyone? Please stay where you are. Jack? Thomas? Ryan? Would you go see what the problem is, please?"

Three uniformed staff members nodded and quickly hurried off. Before they could make it back, though, we all heard what was probably the worst thing anyone wanted to hear in a large gathering of people such as this: calls for a doctor.

One of the staff members was back and he didn't look happy. "We have a problem with the food court, ma'am! There are sick people everywhere! And, I think … I think someone has been killed!"

TWO

S tay here," Vance ordered, as he hurriedly rose to his feet. "Tori? Stay with Zack. I need to go see if there's anything I can do."

"What's going on?" Tori whispered to me. "Do you really think someone has been killed?"

I hooked a thumb at the people rushing by, intent on reaching the exits just as fast as humanly possible.

"They certainly think so. Wow. Had I known there was this much excitement at the big book expos, then I would have signed up long ago."

Movement attracted my attention. Jillian had decided to abandon her place at the front of the audience and join us at our table up on stage. I quickly added a few chairs to the other side of the table, just in case anyone else wanted to join us up here.

"You sure know how to host an event," Jillian teased, as she pulled out the chair on the opposite side of mine and sat down. Both corgis watched us for a little bit before they lowered themselves into down positions and were content to watch the people hurrying by. "What should we do now? Should we leave? And where did Vance go?"

"He left to see about giving the staff a hand," Tori answered. "I'm just hoping he doesn't have to use his police training."

"I just hope no one has died," Jillian said. Tori nodded in agreement. "Nothing is worth losing their life over."

A few uniformed staff members stopped long enough to see that there were still quite a few people in our room.

"We're asking everyone to calmly leave the building. There's nothing to fear. Please follow us."

Calm and orderly it was *not*. The one thing I will say is that panic will very effectively clear a room in no time flat. That was about the time we heard a siren start up in the distance. Then another started wailing. And another. I checked my watch. It was less than ten minutes from the time we heard the first panicked screams, followed almost immediately by the stampede. That's when the second stampede occurred, although this time, it was a good thing.

A steady stream of incoming traffic rolled through the open doors. Teams of paramedics, fire-fighters, policemen, and small groups of what looked like high-ranking officials. The paramedics, each of them carrying orange trauma kits, hurried by. Several of the fire-fighters caught sight of our little group still at the table and paused.

"Is everyone all right?" one of the firemen asked. "No one is hurt?"

"We're good," I assured the emergency personnel. "All the ruckus came from that way. Follow the paramedics."

The fireman gave me a thumbs up and rushed around the corner. Vance reappeared right about then. He saw the three of us seated at the panelist table and veered our way.

"How bad is it?" Jillian asked the moment Vance sat down.

"It's bad," Vance admitted. "I can sadly confirm that one person is dead." He tapped his chest. "There's a small wound right about here. It's too small to be a knife wound, so I'm not sure what caused it."

"And has anyone been poisoned?" I asked.

Vance nodded. "Everywhere I looked, there were people keeled over. Zack? You're definitely gonna want to avoid that area at all costs."

I looked up. "Why?"

"I'm surprised you can't smell it yet. I'm sure you will, soon."

My face paled. Oh. My friend could only be referring to my aversion to vomit. Or, more specifically, the sour, acrid stench associated with it. I was what's known as a *sympathetic puker*. That meant if I saw it, smelled it, or even heard it, then I would more than likely get sick myself.

Vance eyed the bottles of water on the table. Several had been opened, and a few of them were empty.

"Has anyone had anything to eat or drink?"

Thankfully, we all shook our heads no.

"I was about to," I admitted. "My mouth was going dry, and I was reaching for my bottle of water. But, that's about when everything took a turn for the worse. Here it is. See my bottle? It's unopened."

"What about you, Tor?" Vance asked his wife. "Tell me you didn't touch yours, either."

"I didn't," Tori confirmed. "Do you think someone slipped something into the refreshments?"

"I do. Think about it. If someone was stupid enough to release an aerosol-based bug into the air, then everyone would be affected. In this case, no, only people who were in the food court seemed to be affected."

"Heads up," I softly announced. "I think we're about to be interrogated."

We all turned to watch two men approach our table. The man in the lead looked older than me, maybe in his mid-fifties. He had brown hair, balding, and was exceedingly thin, as though he didn't take good enough care of himself. I also noticed how short this fellow was. He had to be no taller than five-foot-four. He had a hooked nose, wore a pair of wire glasses, and had a frown on his face.

My first impression of the guy screamed bachelor to me.

Looking at the second man, I saw that he was younger than his partner, and probably younger than me. He was blond, his skin was fair, and he had high cheekbones. Perhaps he had some Scandinavian blood in him? At any rate, he was taller than his companion, by at least five inches, and was impeccably dressed, as though he was trying to impress his boss. Black slacks, a red Polo shirt, and black sneakers completed the image.

"Good afternoon, folks," the first man said, as the two of them arrived at our table. "I'm Detective Kristofer Martins. This is my consultant, Gregory Plinth. We'd like to ask you some questions, if that's okay with you."

We all nodded.

"We figured you would," Vance said. He pointed at two nearby chairs. "Pull up a seat and join us."

Once the detective and his assistant were seated, Detective Martins pulled out a small notebook and began to write. The consultant had placed his leather bag down and was rifling through it.

"All right. Could I get your names, please?"

We each took turns announcing our names and then spelling them out, just for the record. For those of you who remember, there was a certain someone with us at the moment who did *not* like being left out of introductions. Keeping an eye on Sherlock, I could see that he was waiting for his turn to be acknowledged. When it didn't happen, I saw him growing increasingly anxious. Knowing what was coming, I jammed a finger in each ear. Noticing my actions, and the fact that my three companions had mirrored my movements, the detective cocked his head and stared at me, as though I had sprouted horns.

"What are you …?"

"Wait for it," I interrupted, shaking my head.

A loud, piercing bark sounded from the floor. Surprised, and with their mouths open, both men leaned back and to the side so as to give themselves a better view of the ground. There, staring angrily up at them, was Sherlock.

"By the way," I nonchalantly said, "we have a couple of dogs with us who aren't fans of being ignored. Are your ears bleeding yet? I think mine are. That's all on you, detective."

"Who's this?" Detective Martins asked.

"The one with the black is Sherlock," I said, pointing him out. "The other one is Watson."

"Sherlock and Watson," the detective repeated, smiling. "Cute names. Are they friendly?"

I held a hand out and waited for Sherlock to lick it.

"Incredibly so."

Once *all* the introductions had been made, Detective Martins looked at me.

"Were you sitting here when the ruckus happened next door?"

"Three of us were," I said, nodding. "Myself, Tori, and Vance."

"Did you happen to see anything?" the consultant asked. "I was told you were the one talking when everything went to hell."

"If you knew I was one of the panelists, then why ask if I was sitting up here?"

Martins shrugged and then pointed at the name card in front of my seat. "I would say it's because I didn't notice that. Were you all panelists here?"

I raised a hand. "Actually, it was just me. But, I did drag these two on stage when questions about the book I wrote surfaced. And, before you can ask, I wrote it because of these two. So, yeah, the three of us were up here. Jillian, my fiancée, was sitting over there, in that cordoned-off section. She was holding Sherlock and Watson's leashes. And, for the record, no, I'm sorry. I'm not much of a public speaker, so my eyes were on the table in front of me." When the two men fell silent as they stared at me, I figured I should throw in some context. "It's my coping mechanism. If I don't make eye contact with anyone, then I won't hyperventilate and pass out."

Vance chuckled when he heard this.

"Is he serious?" I heard Tori whisper to Jillian.

"No, of course not. Er, at least, I don't think he is."

"No one noticed anything," Detective Martins said to himself, as he scribbled in his notebook.

The assistant nudged his companion on the arm. "I think you'll find that one of them *did* see something. Ma'am? Am I right in thinking you saw something of interest?"

We all turned to Jillian, who was nodding. "As a matter of fact, I did. How did you know that, Mr. Plinth?"

"You started fidgeting in your chair," Gregory responded. "And call me Greg. It's easier."

Jillian nodded. "Thank you, Greg. I will."

"What did you see?" Detective Martins asked, his pen poised over his notebook.

"Just someone who looked awfully suspicious," Jillian said, as she sat back in her chair.

"What was suspicious about them?" Greg wanted to know.

"From our vantage point here," Jillian began, "we can see the main row of entry doors. That means we can see people coming and going. Now, since this event was in full swing, there was hardly anyone going."

"People were still arriving," Detective Martins said, nodding. He scribbled in his notebook.

Jillian pointed at the bend in the hallway where most of the paying customers to the book show had been headed. "This man in question first appeared there, and headed straight to the front door. You could tell he was in a hurry."

"You said *guy*," Detective Martins observed. "You're sure?"

"Yes. He was wearing a yellow tee shirt, dark jeans, and had one of those things wrapped around his head. Umm, what's it called?"

"A bandana?" I guessed.

Jillian beamed me a smile. "Yes, exactly! He was

wearing a black and gray bandana. I believe he also had on some type of coat. A jacket, maybe?"

"Can you describe him?" Detective Martins hopefully asked. "Height? Weight? Skin color?"

"He looked short," Jillian recalled. "Shorter than me, and I'm five-foot-five. Maybe five-four? He was also lean, but not in a gym-obsessed type of way. Does that make sense?"

Both detective and consultant nodded.

"He had red hair, only ..."

"Only what?" Greg asked, interested.

"It looked very thick, almost clumped together. He might have had dreadlocks."

"Red dreadlocks?"

Jillian nodded, and then placed a hand on her neck. "And tattoos. I saw tattoos all the way up to his chin."

"Next, you'll tell me that he only had one arm," Detective Martins chuckled.

"No, I'm sorry. He had both hands."

"I was joking, ma'am."

"I know you were, detective."

"Do you have any idea how old he was?" Greg asked.

Jillian shrugged. "Oh, gosh, I suppose he was in his mid-twenties."

"That's a very detailed description," Detective Martins admitted, several minutes later. He snapped his notebook closed and looked at Jillian. "Would you care to explain how you were able to be looking in the right place at the right time?"

"She's very observant," I offered. "She always has been. I can never win an argument with her."

Jillian smiled warmly and placed her hand over mine on the table and gave it a friendly squeeze.

"Look, I can vouch for everyone here," Vance began, as he pulled out his police ID. "I'm Detective Vance Samuelson, of the Pomme Valley Police Department. Zack is one of our consultants, as are both Sherlock and Watson."

"Oregon, right?" Detective Martins asked, as he flipped his notebook back open to consult his notes.

"Correct. Zack and the dogs have solved a number of cases for us."

"Have they now? Well, that's nice. Here, in New Orleans, we do everything by the book, Mr. Samuelson."

Vance's smile thinned. "Good to know, Detective Martins. We do the same back home."

Tori laid a reassuring hand on her husband's. "So, detective, what now?"

Martins looked up at the overhead ceiling and noticed several security cameras. He nudged Greg and pointed up.

"Get with the security team here," Detective Martins told the consultant. "Go through the video. Let's see if Ms. Cooper's mystery man shows up in any of the feeds." Greg nodded, but before he could hurry off, Detective Martins held up a hand. "Wait a moment. Let's make sure we cover all the bases. Ma'am? You're the one who has seen the person we're after. Is there any way I could get you to accompany Mr. Plinth here and help him look?"

"Only if all of us can come," Jillian said. "I don't want to be back there by myself."

"Seconded," I added.

Minutes later, we were all following Mr. Plinth as he led us through a number of hallways, before stopping at a black door with a single word written across the front: SECURITY.

"Mr. Dobson, hello again. I have some people here who are going to help us try to locate a person of interest. Er, how much room do you have in there?"

Mr. Dobson, a big, beefy black man who was probably around six and a half feet tall, smiled warmly at us and pulled the door open as much as it could go. I was immediately reminded of a bouncer at a bar.

"Absolutely. We've got room for everyone. Come on in, folks. What's this? Dogs? How cool! They're corgis, aren't they?"

"Pembrokes," I confirmed. "And thanks."

Mr. Dobson returned to his station, in front of at least fifty small screens, and began tapping instructions into the keyboard.

"Now, how far back do you want to go?"

"Well, you have cameras covering the front doors, don't you?" Gregory asked.

Mr. Dobson nodded. "Five."

"Why don't you go back to just before the people panicked," Vance suggested. "That was, what, about an hour ago?"

"Is that when Mr. Anderson pulled you up on stage with him?" the security guard asked, with a smile.

"You know who I am?" I asked, amazed.

"My wife loves that Ireland book you wrote," Mr. Dobson explained. "Now, thanks to you, I gotta find a way to surprise her with a trip to the UK. Can't wait to have a pint of Guinness at an actual Irish bar."

"If you don't mind me asking, Mr. Dobson," I began, "could you tell me how you knew I wrote *Heart of Éire*? Is it written down somewhere?"

The big security tech pulled a duffel bag out from under the table and rifled through it for a few moments. Turning, he was holding a copy of my book in his large hands. He tapped the author name on the cover, namely Jim McGee, and then pointed at a sentence in a smaller font printed just above the name. Leaning forward, I studied the line.

Zachary Anderson, writing as …

Well, I'll be a monkey's uncle. Perhaps I should pay more attention to the cover?

"Ah. Well, that explains a few things. So, uh, have you ever tried Guinness before?"

Dobson shook his head no. "Not yet. Why, have you?"

"Once," I confirmed. "And it will be the last. The texture and flavor of Guinness can be … that is, it could be considered … tell you what. Let's just call it an acquired taste."

"Didn't care for it, huh?" Vance quipped.

"Not one bit. But, people always tell me my taste buds are no better than a bottom-feeder, so I don't think I'm qualified to give a decent opinion."

Dobson laughed and began working his magic on the controls. Much to my surprise, a three-by-three grid of camera feeds in the direct center of the wall of videos fuzzed out and was replaced by an image of the front entry, looking toward the hallway that passed in front of where my panel was. A counter appeared in the lower left corner and counted backwards as Dobson skimmed through the footage. We watched hundreds of people jump about in reverse as Dobson searched for the correct time frame. Then, the people seemingly vanished and the picture went still.

I stared at the huge wall full of different screens and realized something. All these screens? They were essentially part of the same massive video screen. I'm pretty sure I was looking at the largest computer monitor I've ever seen. Whatever computer program was using it had divided the surface area up to display as many feeds as (presumably) the user wanted. That was one way to get the most bang for your buck.

"I think I've got something," Dobson reported, bringing me back to reality. "This is about five minutes before everything went south."

"Go forward, but slowly," Gregory instructed.

Several figures appeared and quickly accelerated. We watched as three minutes passed in about twenty seconds. Then, as we approached the five minute mark, Jillian suddenly grabbed my arm and pointed at the screen.

"There! Stop the footage! That's him! Zachary, do you see him?"

We all crowded close to the monitors, which I later learned wasn't one big LCD screen, but a series of frameless displays set so close together that they could be used as one giant screen if the situation called for it. A lone figure appeared, and Jillian was right: yellow shirt, black jacket, black jeans, and bright red hair. He was clearly heading for the entrance.

"So, this is who you saw?" Gregory said, as he studied the image. "Can we trace this back? Where did he come from?"

"Let's find out," Dobson muttered, as his hands flew across the keyboard.

The mini videos on the huge screen suddenly turned black. Then, every one of them had an image playing. I nodded as I realized what I was looking at. Dobson was now playing all the video, recorded from each camera, on its own separate feed. We just had to watch the cameras and find out which way our mystery man had come from.

"His hair is, without a doubt, red," Tori observed. "And it does look like dreadlocks to me."

The image suddenly froze. Dead-centered on the screen was a crystal clear picture of our suspect. His back was to the camera, which wasn't ideal, but his head was turned to the left. A blinking blue rectangle appeared, and was resized so that it fit over the suspect's head and torso. Moments later, the image was replaced by a close-up of our perp.

"They're hanging halfway down the guy's back," Vance pointed out.

"But, are they dreadlocks?" I wanted to know.

Vance, Tori, and Jillian all turned to look at me.

"What?" I demanded, growing defensive.

"You need glasses, pal," Vance told me. "We can all see that they're dreadlocks."

"Says the man who isn't wearing his own glasses," Tori quipped.

Surprised, I turned to my friend.

"They're reading glasses," Vance grumbled. "And I forgot to bring them with me on this trip."

Tori reached into her purse and pulled out a brown leather eyeglasses holder. "I figured you might, so I brought your spare pair for you."

Jillian and I were silent as Vance reluctantly donned his eyewear. Avoiding eye contact with me, he leaned forward and studied the image again.

Now it was Jillian's turn to point. "There, see? Can you see his neck? It's covered with tattoos."

"Roger that," Greg said, as he made some of his own notes. "Mr. Dobson, is there any way you can zoom in on the guy's neck? I'd like to see if we can identify any of the images."

Vance and Tori both leaned forward at the same time, and cracked their heads together.

I pulled out my phone. "Guys? Could you do that again? I'd like to film it this time."

Vance rubbed his head. "Bite me, pal."

Tori massaged the side of her head. "Well, I can see a skull, located about here." She tapped an area under her left ear. "And it looks like there might be UFOs for eyes?"

"Suns," Vance corrected.

"Those aren't suns," Tori argued. "We're going to get you some stronger glasses. Those are UFOs."

The image we were staring at suddenly expanded in size and filled the screen. What we were looking at was a crystal clear close-up of the victim's neck. Granted, our friend Mr. Dreadlocks wasn't walking around, shirtless, but enough of his neck was exposed where we could see that he had undoubtedly spent a pretty penny at a tattoo parlor.

I looked at the tattoo of the skull. No, the eyes weren't UFOs, or even suns. In fact, I thought they looked an awful lot like … I don't know. Pancakes?

"If you want to put the UFOs or suns debate to bed once and for all," my detective friend said, "then listen up. It's neither. The skull's eyes are buttons."

I reflexively leaned forward once more. "Really? I thought they were something completely different."

Vance removed his glasses and held them out to

me. "Wanna borrow 'em? Looked like you could've used them earlier."

"Hmmph. They look better on you."

Dobson leaned forward to stare at the screen. "I can enlarge this one. Hold on. Yes, look at that. They're buttons, all right."

"Which way is he heading?" Vance asked.

"It's in reverse," I pointed out. "We're trying to find out where he came from."

"Fine. Find out where he was prior to walking through that hallway, there, on the way out."

"The food court," Dobson reported. "That hallway will take you straight to the food court. Look at that screen, top left. You can see him loitering there, by the Chinese food place, and then, prior to that, he was over by the sandwich shop."

"Is there anything else we can tell about the guy?" Plinth wanted to know.

"He sure is going out of his way to stand out," I mumbled.

"What do you mean?" Vance asked. He leaned forward for a better look. "I mean, sure, he's got red dreadlocks. Not many people can pull off that look."

"I'm not sure *he* is able to pull that one off," Tori observed.

"Look at him," I urged. I stood and leaned over to point at the video feed that had our guy. "Dreadlocks is wearing a bandana, black pants, boots, and a bright yellow shirt. Plus, he's got on a black duster. That's about the equivalent of windowless cargo van driving through a school yard."

"You're suggesting he wanted to be noticed," Vance guessed, as he stared at the image.

"It's just an opinion," I said, as I stepped away from the monitors. "I just don't know why he'd want to, unless he was looking to get captured."

"I'd be more interested in learning about the veve," Jillian said.

"The what?" Vance asked, as he turned to look at my fiancée.

"I have no idea what she said, either," I had to admit. "What is a vay-vay?"

"Veves are used in voodoo," Dobson said, nodding. "You're right, ma'am. I see it, too."

I peered closely at Dreadlocks' neck. All I could see was a jumble of images. Hearts, stars, skulls, boobs, and babes. All were represented on Dreadlocks' neck and all were smooshed together. And Jillian, without bothering to lean forward, had spotted something in that mess which had some meaning?

I pointed at the screen. "Can you bring this veve thing up so that those of us who know nothing about voodoo can see what these things look like?"

Dobson was nodding. "Sure, just a second."

The blue rectangle reappeared. Dobson dragged the box over to Dreadlocks' neck and zoomed the image in even further. It took several more magnifications before I spotted what had caught Jillian's eye. Surprising myself on how quickly it happened, I pulled my cell from my pocket in one fluid motion and snapped a picture of the image frozen on the security screen. I figured I could always study the image later.

It was a symbol, all right, but not something I ever recall seeing. And, let's be honest. If I ever saw something like this in passing, I know I would either laugh it off or flat-out ignore it. In this case, this particular symbol had been set into the top of one of the skulls, directly below the suspect's left ear. Unless you knew what you were looking for, you'd just pass it off as an artist being creative. But, in this case, Jillian had zeroed in on it instantly. Plus, our pal Dobson here confirmed it had something to do with voodoo.

Now, would something like that catch your attention? This *veve* consisted of two overlapping arrows, one pointing northwest, and the other northeast. Tiny stars were at all four points of the compass, and there was also a zig-zag going through the middle of the arrows. No, wait. It actually looked like a backwards *Z*. Or a backwards *N*, tilted about 45 degrees clockwise. I guess it would depend on how you looked at it. Additionally, there was something on the tip of the squiggly line, directly above the southern star. What was it? Well, I certainly didn't know the technical name of it, so I guess I'll call it a hook, or maybe a barb. Now you know as much as I do about this particular symbol. If this thing had some sort of meaningful purpose, it was lost on me.

Vowing to look the crazy thing up once we made it back to our hotel, I was about to ask if there was anything else of note. However, Sherlock and Watson chose that time to wake up from their nap and sniff the air, as though they were able to smell food. Let's face it, they probably were. Then again, they'd been sleeping for a little while. Perhaps they needed a potty break?

"Hey, there's somethin'," Mr. Dobson suddenly reported. He pointed at one of the screens. "There? Did you see that? He's standin' there, by the sandwich shop."

Vance perked up. "He dropped something by that cement planter. Could anyone see what it was?"

"Maybe a wallet?" I suggested. Everyone in the room was staring at me as though they thought I was the biggest dunce of them all. And, I'm sorry to say, that included the dogs. "What? It could be, couldn't it?"

"Not on purpose," Vance decided. "Come on. I want to find out what that thing is. Mr. Plinth? What do you say?"

"I say I'll be right behind you," Greg said.

"It's good timing," I decided. "I think they may need to go out to go potty. It's been a few hours since either of them were outside."

Vance shook his head. "I'd say they want to go

find this thing, too. I mean, look at them. Sherlock and Watson perked up just moments before we saw the footage of the guy dropping whatever it was he dropped. And now? They don't want to go outside, but around that corner. Zack, they want to check out the food court!"

"Fine. Guys? Let's go see if we can find this thing. Remember, look but don't touch, okay?"

Giving the corgis as much leash as I could, I followed them down the hall and into the indoor courtyard. Several crime scene techs were still poking about here and there, taking samples, pictures, notes, and whatever else you could think of. Several police officers eyed us as we neared, but thanks to Vance, and him flashing his police badge, we were allowed through.

"Keep them clear of those areas over there," the nearest cop said, pointing at several tables which had no fewer than four different techs examining the scene.

We looked down at the dogs, who were eyeing one of four large potted ferns. It certainly looked like the planter from the video. Before I could say anything, the dogs guided us to the closest planter, looked up at the large plant, and whined. Sherlock looked back at me and immediately plunked his butt down.

"All right, Sherlock!" Vance praised. He approached the plant and, using an empty serving tray procured from a stack of empties on a nearby trash can, gently moved a few of the fronds out of the way.

"Do you see anything?" I eagerly asked.

Vance suddenly froze, stooped to get a better look at something, and then looked over at the closest crime scene tech.

"Hey, guys? Could I get one of you to come over here, please?"

The tech in question, a young woman in her late twenties, pulled off her latex gloves and headed toward us.

"Yes? Can I help you with something?"

"I think we might be able to help *you* with something," Vance countered, as he pointed at the fern. "Would you look in there and tell me what you see? And I'd put on another pair of gloves, if I were you."

Baffled, the woman looked at the fern, back at Vance, and then over at Gregory Plinth, who nodded his encouragement. Snapping on another pair of gloves, she gently pulled a few fronds out of the way. Right then, she let out an exclamation of surprise.

"Bill? Griff? Guys, you need to see this."

"Is it in there?" I repeated, growing more curious by the second. "What is it? Can you tell?"

The woman gingerly reached into the heart of the plant and pulled out something the size of her hand. She held it up for all to see.

It was a voodoo doll, complete with several pins stuck in various places.

THREE

Tell me it's just a child's toy," I said, addressing the lady tech. "It's just a fluke, isn't it? You can't possibly tell me that doll is the real thing."

The woman shrugged. Holding the doll between her thumb and forefinger, she studied it for a few moments before dropping it into an empty evidence bag, but not before I managed to snap a picture of it.

"Whether it is, or isn't, we're not going to take any chances. We'll see if we can recover any DNA from the doll. Was there anything else?"

I looked down at the dogs. Was there?

"Is there anything else you want us to look at in here, guys?"

"You're talking to your dogs as though they can understand you," the woman said to me, wearing a puzzled frown.

"It'd take too long to explain," I chuckled. "Let's

just say both Sherlock and Watson are way more observant than I'll ever be."

"Does anyone else want to get some lunch?" Vance casually asked.

Jillian, Tori, and I all turned, with the same expression on our faces.

"What?" Vance sputtered, growing defensive. "Isn't anyone else hungry? I haven't had anything since breakfast, and certainly don't want to get anything here."

"People were poisoned," Tori reminded him. "We don't know if they're going to survive."

I snapped my fingers. "And someone might've been run through with ... with ..."

"A large jousting pole?" Vance dryly asked. "Voodoo is just a load of malarkey."

I shook my head. "It really isn't. It's a legitimate religion, practiced by an estimated sixty million people."

"You made that up," Vance accused.

"I really didn't," I admitted. "I looked it up once I saw the voodoo doll."

"Sixty million?" Jillian repeated. "I did not know that."

"Neither did I," Tori added.

I raised a hand. "I'll willingly join the club. I never would have dreamed there were so many people who practice voodoo on a daily basis. Makes you wonder just how authentic it is, doesn't it?"

Vance hooked a thumb back in the direction of the food court. "You're wondering if the person who died back there was also jabbed through the heart? I think that would be the mother of all coincidences."

My arms were folded across my chest. "You said someone died back there. What if … what if there was a teeny, tiny puncture wound on the chest? Would that not suggest …?"

"I did see blood on the guy's chest," Vance confirmed. "But, that doesn't mean he died because some doll was stuck with a couple of pins. Tell you what. If it turns out that …"

"Really?" Tori interrupted. "You're making another wager with Zack? Don't you recall what happened last time?"

Tori was referring to the mother of all Kodak moments, when—as a result of losing a wager about a missing Egyptian pendant—Vance had agreed to don a Peter Pan outfit, complete with matching tights, and take a tap dancing class. That particular video still rakes in hundreds of new views daily on the Internet.

"Yeah, all right, maybe not," Vance conceded. "All I'm trying to say is that we shouldn't jump to conclusions."

Ten minutes later, we were walking along Royal Street. Granted, Bourbon Street was much more popular, but then again, that was also why we *weren't* taking it. There had to be at least four times as many people milling about as there were on Royal. Plus, Jillian had found a nice little café with an outdoor pet-friendly patio there, called Café

Beignet. My fiancée had sold me on the restaurant the moment she had read me the definition of beignet: a French donut.

As we approached the front entrance of the restaurant, we stopped just outside the front doors and inspected the menus, which were set into a display on the wall.

"Oooh, this looks good, Zachary. I'll bet that mushroom omelet is fantastic. What about you? Do you see anything you like?"

"Quite a few," I said, nodding. "This ham and cheese omelet looks good, as does the French toast, the Belgian waffle, or maybe ..."

"Guys?" Vance interrupted. "It's lunchtime."

"Oh." My gaze dropped several inches to look at the lunch offerings. "Well, we have some good-looking sandwiches. The Royal Croissant looks good. I think I'll order that. Jillian? What about you? I think you'd like ... what are the dogs doing? Sherlock? This stuff isn't for you, pal."

"What's he doing?" Vance asked, as he leaned around me to look at the corgis.

I pointed at the menu. "If I didn't know any better, then I'd say he wants to order something, too."

Both Sherlock and Watson had reared up on their hind legs, with their front legs resting on the wall, in an effort to get closer to the menus. My curiosity finally won me over. I stooped to pick up Sherlock and I held him next to the menus.

"I can't believe I'm doing this. There. You see, Sherlock? There's nothing here but a simple, boring menu. It's nothing a corgi would like."

"Awwwwooooooo," Sherlock argued, uttering a low howl.

"There must be something on the menu that he wants us to notice," Jillian decided.

"We're not working a case," I reminded her.

Jillian shrugged. "Tell that to *them*."

"Fine. There. I took a picture of the menu. Will that appease Your Royal Highnesses?"

Both dogs immediately settled down. Shaking my head, my phone was returned to my pocket, and I waited outside while Jillian and Tori headed inside to see about getting a table. Once we were comfortably sitting outside on Café Beignet's patio, Jillian held up her glass of lemonade and smiled at the three of us.

"Here's to New Orleans, and to Zachary, for making this all possible."

I held up my glass of soda and nodded at Vance. "Here's to Vance for suggesting one helluva idea."

Tori, knowing full well that Vance should be the next to raise his glass and offer his thanks, presumably to me, elbowed him in the gut and held her lemonade up, expectantly. My friend sighed, reached for his own lemonade, and held it up.

"All right, fine. Here's to Zack, for being a good writer and a better friend. Thanks for including us."

I clinked my glass against his. "You're welcome, amigo. And, for the record, that sounded painful. Was it?"

Vance laughed. "You have no idea."

"So, who has never had a beignet before?" Jillian eagerly asked, after a waitress appeared and set down the tray of donut appetizers.

I raised a hand. "I don't recall ever eating these things before."

Jillian pushed my hand down. "You had some at Disneyland with me last year. Granted, they were shaped like Mickey Mouse, but they were just as tasty. Still don't remember? You ordered the pumpkin-flavored one."

Ah, now it clicked, and I'm sure my face lit up.

"Oh, I remember that pumpkin donut thing. You're right. It was very good."

"Have either of you guys ever been to Café Du Monde?" Tori asked. "I hear their beignets are really good, too."

I was shaking my head no, but I stopped when I saw Jillian nodding.

"These are better," Jillian was saying. "The beignets at Café Du Monde are smaller and crispier. These ones are much larger, and as a result, they're softer."

The waitress stopped by to top off our (nearly) empty glasses. A pitcher of lemonade was produced, and promptly left on the table after three of the glasses were filled. Mine was the only odd one out, since it had soda in it. But, before I could say anything, a second glass of soda appeared next to my empty one. Smiling my thanks, I noticed the small leather pouch swinging from the waitress' neck.

It looked homemade to me. The pouch was about the size of a silver dollar. It was made of a dark leather, with a lighter color cord forming the pouch. A mixture of small red and green beads were sewn onto the center of the pouch, creating a geometric design. The waitress caught me staring and gently clasped the pouch in her hand.

"Do you like it? I made it myself."

Both corgis were watching the waitress intently.

"I do. If you made that, then you did a great job."

"It's my own version of a gris-gris. It's my good luck charm. You can find them for sale just about everywhere around here."

I held up a hand. "Okay, what did you call that thing? A gris-gris?"

"It's an amulet," the waitress explained. "It protects the wearer from evil."

I nodded. "Good to know." After the waitress moved off, I leaned forward. Anticipating I wanted to share something, but only with the three of them, Vance, Tori, and Jillian leaned forward, too. "Let me ask you guys something. That voodoo doll the dogs found? Do you think it has anything to do with that … that … you know what? I don't remember what it was called. Jillian? That voodoo symbol thingamajig? What was it called?"

"A veve."

I snapped my fingers. "Right. A veve. It's clearly symbolic, and since we found that doll, I can't stop thinking about how much I really *don't* know about anything and everything voodoo. And that good luck charm the waitress was wearing? Would anyone like to wager on whether or not it has some type of a voodoo connection?"

Jillian pointed northeast. "If you're interested, Zachary, Marie Laveau's House of Voodoo is about two blocks that way."

"House of Voodoo?" I slowly repeated. "Seriously?"

Tori was nodding. "Oh, yeah, it's world famous."

I looked at Vance, who shrugged. It would appear the good detective knew just as much about Marie Laveau as I did. Mistaking my silence as reluctance, Jillian pulled up the store's website and showed it to me on her phone. What I saw had my eyebrows jumping straight up.

This store was jam packed full of some of the strangest things I had ever laid eyes on. A bright, colorful assortment of masks was hanging on one wall. On another, I could see what looked like a selection of various shrunken heads. Then, unsurprisingly since this *was* New Orleans after all, I saw rows and rows of beaded necklaces. Racks of clothing, emblazoned with the store logo and the Marie Laveau name in every creepy font imaginable hung on pegs on the opposite wall. Pamphlets, books, and brochures were situated near the cashier. And, I should mention that, everywhere I looked, I could see strange scribbles, designs, and pictographs. Jillian told me later that they were, in fact, more examples of veves.

Long rectangular glass display cases ran the length of the store on the left, and in them? Tiny figurines, multi-sided die, flashy trinkets, bits of jewelry, and decks of Tarot cards. That was just one of the display cases I could see. In an adjacent case, I saw all manner of dolls, complete with convenient packs of assorted pins to accompany them. For the record, the picture was too small to tell if the voodoo doll we had found had been sold from this store.

Incredible. The more I looked, the more I felt a headache brewing. Then again, I think that was because the store was so bizarre, and there were so many things to look at, that my eyes kept jumping around, as if I couldn't decide what I should be focusing my attention on. But, with that being said, I was nodding my head long before Jillian suggested we should stop by. I don't care if that place gave me the mother of all migraines. I wanted to go.

Tori pulled up the same website on her phone so she could show Vance.

"What do you think?" Vance asked me, after he had silently studied the phone for nearly five minutes. "Do you think this place is legit, or do you think it just caters to tourists?"

"Probably a bit of both," I decided. "We just have to hope there's someone there who knows what they're talking about."

Twenty minutes later, we were walking along

Royal Street, chatting about the events of the day, when the dogs pulled me to a stop. Conversations died off as the four of us watched Sherlock and Watson—in unison—sniff the air. Making sure I wasn't being watched, I did the same.

"Are they *H*?" Jillian softly asked.

I checked the time on my phone. "They've got a few hours, so they should be good. Although, in their defense, whatever that is sure smells good."

Jillian delicately sniffed the air.

"Smells like some type of soup. Based on the ingredients I can smell, I can most certainly recommend you don't try it, Zachary."

"It doesn't smell too bad," I admitted.

"I can smell spinach, artichokes, and lima beans."

"You can smell all of that? Good thing we already had lunch. Ah. Look, they must be smelling this place, the Crawfish Shack."

The four of us hesitated as we passed a small wooden shack with its front doors wide open. Well, it certainly looked as though it lived up to its name.

"If they're *hambre*," Vance quietly said, as though my dogs could understand Spanish and could figure out someone had just said hungry, "then why didn't they react to the last two restaurants we passed? Why show any interest in this one?"

I looked at the restaurant. This one, according to the sign, specialized in crawfish. I looked at

Vance and shrugged. Tugging the leashes, we returned to the sidewalk, anxious to be on our way. At least, that's what I *tried* to do. Both leashes became taut as I realized neither dog had budged an inch.

"Guys? Come on. We're headed *that way*."

Sherlock looked at me and tilted his head, as though I had just made a strange noise. Jillian pointed at a nearby sign.

"Look, Zachary. It's their menu. Do you see anything that stands out?"

I checked the restaurant's offerings. I would definitely *not* be eating here. Crawfish cakes, crawfish burger, raw crawfish, crawfish stuffed salad, crawfish soup, and even crawfish gumbo. *Blech.*

"Just a whole lot of crawfish dishes I never knew existed. Really, guys? Are you telling me you want to try their crawfish?"

There's nothing quite like when your dogs look at you and you *know* they think you're the stupidest thing on two legs. In this case, Sherlock was staring at me with a look on his face which said, *Really?*

Sighing, I pulled out my cell and snapped a few shots, being sure to include the name of the place, the building, and then the menu. Even before I could ask, both corgis were on their feet and eager to resume their walk.

Dogs.

Ten minutes later, we found the voodoo place, and oh what a place it was. Once again, my eyes darted from wall to wall, from counter to floor, from floor to ceiling. Every available square inch of surface space had something on it. In fact, most had *two* somethings.

"My, my, what 'ave we 'ere?" a chipper woman in her late thirties asked, once we stepped foot into Marie Laveau's House of Voodoo. She was tastefully dressed in a violet blouse and black slacks, and had her long brown hair pulled up and away from her face. "You not from around 'ere, are you?"

There was an accent on the woman's voice, only I couldn't place it. No, scratch that. It wasn't how she was speaking, since I could understand her completely, but the way she was saying the words. After a few moments, it came to me. I know what she's doing. She was leaving some letters out, but even after omitting parts of the sentence, I could still follow along.

"Good afternoon," I said, as I approached the counter. "And you're right. We are not from around here. In fact, the four of us are from Oregon."

"Or'gon?" the woman repeated, grinning. "What you doin' all the way out 'ere?"

"Zachary is a writer," Jillian explained. "We were at a book signing when things became, uh, a little crazy."

"Is that where the police 'eaded? Saw cop cars tear up the street a few 'ours ago."

"That was it," Jillian confirmed. She held out a hand. "I'm Jillian Cooper. I love your shop."

The woman took my fiancée's hand and smiled.

"Brittany Macarty. You can call me Britt."

"It's lovely to meet you, Britt," Jillian returned. "This is my fiancé, Zachary. Over there are our good friends, Vance and Tori Samuelson. And finally, before I forget, down there are Sherlock and Watson."

Brittany raised up on her tiptoes to look over the counter. When she spotted the corgis, she grinned. "Thought I 'eard dog collars. Hello down there."

Sherlock and Watson craned their necks to look up at the friendly clerk.

"Thanks for allowing them in here," I said. "Not many places are dog friendly."

"No food served here," Britt told us. "Clean up after them, then there no problem 'ere."

I pulled up the picture of the voodoo doll Sherlock found on my phone. I held it up in a questioning manner.

"Can you tell us anything about this?"

Britt took my phone and studied the picture.

"Well, each doll is different. You expecting rules? Nope. No rules. Dolls 'ave different functions."

Vance and Tori wandered close. Brittany began counting off her fingers.

"First, we 'ave love. Ninety-percent of all dolls be asking for 'elp with love."

"Like, I want this person to fall in love with me?" Vance asked.

"You'd think that, but no," Brittany said, shaking her head. "Most common be the return of a lover."

"You learn something new every day," I whispered to Jillian, who promptly shushed me.

"Second most popular?" Brittany said, looking at the four of us. "Keeping faithful."

"What about the pins?" I asked. "If you say most dolls are used for love, then why do we always find these things skewered with long pins?"

Britt shook her head with disgust. "American television and movies always mess up the facts. A pin on a doll doesn't mean someone wants you dead. It means something attached to the doll."

"To make it resemble the person it's supposed to be mimicking," Jillian guessed.

Brittany nodded. "That's right. So, this picture? You can't really see where the pins stuck. Chest? Shoulders? Maybe on the 'ead? Can't tell."

"Do you think there's a chance this isn't legit?" Vance asked.

Brittany was shaking her head. "Voodoo dolls come in many shapes and sizes. The question I'd be asking is, these pins 'ere?"

"What about them?" Vance asked.

"I'd want to know where they 'ad been inserted. Was there anything pinned with 'em? Were they 'olding something in place on the doll? Scrap of clothing? Piece of 'air?"

Vance pulled out his phone. "I can check with Detective Martins."

"You have his number?" I quietly asked. "Should

you be bothering him? We're not officially on the case, you know."

Vance produced a business card. "If he didn't want me bothering him, then he shouldn't have given me his number."

"Take it outside," Tori softly told him.

Vance nodded and headed for the door.

"Are gris-gris's … gris-grisses … is a gris-gris … do you know what a gris-gris is?"

Brittany nodded. "Voodoo talisman. Most are good luck charms, or used to ward off evil."

"Do you sell them here?" I asked.

Brittany turned and, holding out her hand, swung it in an arch directly behind her. "We have them, yes we do. Int'rested?"

I nodded. "I'm finding this stuff fascinating. Sure, I'll take one. Jillian? Would you like a good luck charm?"

Jillian smiled. "I never turn down good luck charms."

I then heard a very distinctive noise: the shaking of a collar. Looking down, I saw Sherlock slowly looking around the store. His eyes had locked on something and he had started moving toward it. Looking over at Jillian, I shrugged, and held out the leashes. My fiancée took possession of both dogs and wandered off while I made my purchases.

"Ah! Oya!"

I had just slipped my phone into my pocket and was in the process of turning around when Brittany had called out the strange word. Turning, I could see she was pointing at my pocket.

"What was that?"

"You carry the mark of Oya, only you don't seem the type."

"I don't know what *Oya* is, but I can tell you I certainly am not carrying his or her mark."

"I saw it on your telephone. Do you mind? May I see it again?"

"What, my phone? Yeah, sure. What is an oyo, anyway?"

I unlocked my phone and placed it on the counter. There, on the screen, was a picture. Fumble-fingers here must have held something down a little too long, because somehow, my photos app had been loaded and a picture was displayed. This one was of the veve Jillian had spotted on our mystery man's neck. I had forgotten the symbol was sitting on my phone.

"*Oya*," Brittany corrected, throwing some emphasis behind the word. "Warrior-goddess. She who 'as the power to unleash the storms. She 'as the power to sweep all injustice, dis'onesty, and deceit from her path."

"Umm, is that a good thing or a bad thing?" I asked. "That could almost be taken either way."

Brittany was nodding. "She be impulsive. She can be benevolent mother or unpredictable warrior. You don't disrespect Oya."

"And that's her symbol?" I asked, as I pointed at my phone and the close-up of the veve on the skull tattoo.

"Aye. Oya she is called the Mother of Nine. She be most powerful of orishas."

"Orishas?" I asked. I had pulled the mini notebook I kept with me at all times and was scribbling notes. "What are they?"

"Orishas be representatives of Olodumare, the Supreme Being," Brittany explained, as she rang me up for the two amulets I had chosen. "Olodumare placed orishas on Earth to supervise and 'elp mankind."

"As far as us humans are concerned, these orishas? They're essentially gods?"

Brittany nodded. "More like demi-gods, but aye. Oya brings rapid change."

I finished writing my notes and nodded. Vance was going to want to hear this. Brittany handed me my purchases and I nodded my thanks. Spotting Jillian and the dogs standing near Tori at the back of the store, I headed their way. I was eager to tell them the veve Jillian had spotted in the video footage had been identified, but before I could say anything, my own phone started to ring.

"Hello?"

"Mr. Anderson?" a strange voice asked.

"Yes. Who's this?"

"You're Zachary Anderson, the writer?"

"You're two for two," I told the voice. "You know about me. Do I know you?"

"Hmm? Oh, I'm sorry. This is Gregory Plinth. We met earlier today, at the expo center? Do you remember me?"

"Well, it was only a couple of hours ago, Mr. Plinth. Of course I remember you."

"Thank you, Mr. Anderson. You can call me Greg."

"If we're dropping formalities, then you can call me Zack."

"Zack … got it. Listen, Zack, I have what might be an unusual request for you."

"Hey, isn't Vance talking to Detective Martins right now?" I curiously asked. "Last I heard, he had some questions about the voodoo doll we found."

"I'm not with Detective Martins at the moment," Greg confessed. "I was actually meeting with Captain Donnelly."

"How long have you been a consultant?" I wanted to know.

"A few years. Why do you want to know?"

"As it turns out, I'm one, too."

"You are? Have you applied to the police academy, too? They keep rejecting me. Flat feet. Go figure, huh?"

"I'm not trying to become a full-time cop," I said, shaking my head. "No desires there. Consider yourself fortunate. You're here because they value your opinion. Whenever I'm called out on a case, it's because they want me to hold a couple of leashes."

Greg laughed. "So, there's something you need to know about Captain Donnelly."

"I don't know who that is," I admitted.

JEFFREY POOLE

"He's Detective Martins' boss. Well, he'd be my boss, too, if they ever paid me for my time here. Anyway, the captain was curious about the work you do for Pomme Valley and did some research."

I chuckled. "He learned about Sherlock and Watson's previous cases, didn't he?"

"He got on the phone with one Chief Nelson."

"Chief Nelson," I repeated. "I know him well."

"He spoke very highly of you and your dogs," Gregory said.

I wonder what he would say if he knew Chief Nelson once suspected me of murder.

"So, your captain talked to my captain. Did Captain Donnelly learn what he wanted to know?"

"That and more," Gregory confirmed. "He'd like your help, Zack."

"Say again?" I asked, certain I had misheard. "Why would your police captain want my help? New Orleans is a huge city. I'm sure you have plenty of detectives and investigators to do this sort of thing."

"You and your dogs wouldn't be officially working the case," Gregory clarified. "Everything will be done without anyone knowing about it, *but* with the full cooperation of the NOPD. What do you say?"

"I'd say that you guys are all crazy. I'm an author. I'm here for a book convention."

"I'm sorry to say that the convention has been put on hold," Gregory sadly informed me. "That means you'll have some free time on your hands, doesn't it?"

"Then, I'd much rather look around and make like a tourist. I'm here with some friends of mine, along with my fiancée and my dogs. The last thing they're gonna want to hear is that I'm working a case."

"I have a message from Chief Nelson," Gregory suddenly announced.

Oh, swell.

"Great. Let's hear it."

"Mr. Anderson, I have a lot of faith in you. Check with Vance. I think you'll find that there's a lot riding on this. Make us proud."

"There's a lot riding on this?" I repeated.

"Captain Donnelly and Chief Nelson might have made a, uh, wager regarding the outcome of this case."

My eyes widened. "They bet on us. Let me guess. Chief Nelson is betting we can solve it before you guys do."

Gregory laughed. "That is the gist of the wager, yes."

"And the stakes?"

"They wouldn't tell me."

Vance suddenly strode back in the store, with a look of incredulity on his face. "Dude, you're not going to believe this. I just heard from … oh, my bad. I didn't see you were on the phone."

I held up a finger, signaling my friend to wait. "I've got the consultant on the phone. He was just telling me something about a bet."

Vance nodded. "That's right. Zack? We're on the case. We've got to solve this thing before they do!"

FOUR

Y ou have to explain this to me," I was saying. "Here we are, walking down world-
famous Bourbon Street in New Orleans, and somehow, we've been corralled into working a case?"

"Call it a collaboration between our two police
departments," Vance suggested.

Shaking my head, I frowned. "We're here because of the Ireland book, remember? We're on
MCU's dime."

"But, there's nothing going on right now,"
Vance protested. "You said so yourself."

"Yeah, I did," I confirmed. "But, what happens
when they call up and say, all right, instead of attending a panel *there*, we're going to need you to
come over *here*? I'm not sure I feel comfortable
doing this."

"Let's look at it this way," Vance began. "If MCU
calls up and wants you to attend some other function, then no worries. We'll drop what we're doing

and rush over."

We navigated our way around a group of street vendors, who immediately swarmed us as they tried to persuade us to buy their merchandise. Vance flashed them his badge and they immediately scattered.

"You shouldn't be doing that," Tori scolded. "They're just trying to make a living."

"I hate salesmen," Vance grumbled.

Tori nodded. "I know. Let it go, okay?"

"Can you tell us about this wager?" Jillian asked. "How is it the captain of the local police department here happens to know Chief Nelson back home?"

"He doesn't," Vance reported. "But, he was curious about Zack and the dogs. So, they looked up Pomme Valley and, seeing how our town isn't that big, were easily able to pull up a phone number. The two of them got to talking and someone—and I don't know who—said this has the makings of a spectacular wager."

"How did they convince you to get on board?" I asked. "I mean, you took time off to come here, didn't you?"

"I did," Vance said. "Chief Nelson said he'll make it up to me in some fashion."

"Tell him what else he promised," Tori urged.

"Oh. The captain also said …"

"Just a minute," I interrupted. "I've heard you call him Chief Nelson, and just now, captain. Which is it?"

"Technically, he's Captain Nelson," Vance answered. "But, he prefers Chief Nelson. It's a preference, I guess. Just go with it. I always do."

"Right. So, what did Chief Nelson promise you if we solve this case before the New Orleans cops do?"

"About thirty grand."

My eyebrows shot up. "Wow, are you serious?"

Vance shrugged. "There might be a change in job title, too."

Jillian smiled and nodded. "He's offering you a promotion, isn't he?"

"If we can get this case solved before the locals, then yes, I will become Senior Detective," Vance confirmed.

I gave my friend a congratulatory slap on the back. "Dude, nice! Although, if you ask me, I think you should have been awarded that title years ago."

"Seconded," Tori quietly added.

"What about Zachary?" Jillian asked, as she turned back to Vance. "You get a job promotion, but Zachary is only a civilian. He's a consultant. There's not much the chief can do for him, is there?"

Vance groaned. "I knew we were gonna get around to this sooner or later. Yes, there are some incentives for you, too, Zack. Since he's not here, I can simply say Chief Nelson is one evil son of a ... oof!"

Tori had punched him in the stomach.

"Don't finish that statement. Your language is

already foul enough. Besides, you promised the girls you'd try and refrain from using all profanity."

"Fine," Vance grumbled. My friend looked back at me. "Chief Nelson said that if you were to play along, and actually get Sherlock and Watson to solve this thing before the locals, then … oh, man. I can't make myself say it."

Tori brightened. "But *I* can. Guys? Apparently Chief Nelson is a huge fan of YouTube. He loves watching all those funny videos. Well, he admitted to finding Vance's Peter Pan video, and wants to see him do something else."

My scowl was gone in a flash.

"Oh, really? You have my attention. If I cooperate, what does Vance have to do?"

"Oh, nothing much, just shave his head and perform a very popular song from a Disney movie. While being recorded, of course."

I snatched up the dogs' leashes. "Done. Let's go solve this thing, shall we?"

"You didn't hear what song he has to sing!" Tori protested.

"Does it matter?" I returned. I looked at my friend. "How in the world did the chief get you to go along with this?"

"By dangling the promotion in front of him," Jillian guessed.

Vance sulked and stared at the floor.

"Is this sort of thing ethical?" I inquired. "I mean, can the chief really push Vance to do this?"

Vance scowled again. "Not really. Then again, he made a show of pointing out everything was voluntary. If I choose to do this, and earn fame and accolade for PV, then I would be rewarded by earning a new title."

"Are you totally willing to do this?" I quietly asked.

"Dude, did you hear the part about the pay raise?" Vance quietly reminded me.

"I did, but are you forgetting the royalty checks the book keeps bringing in?"

"Not at all. Do we know how much longer the book will continue to sell? It's an uncertainty. This promotion isn't. So, if all goes well, then I'll be sporting a new *do*, and looking up the lyrics to some song called *Let it Go*."

"You haven't seen *Frozen*?" Jillian asked, dumbfounded. "You have two adorable little girls. I thought for certain you would have watched that movie with them."

"The two princesses who are sisters?" Vance asked. "Sure, I remember that one. Isn't one an ice queen? In fact, I … oh, no! Why on earth didn't I remember that blasted song? Omigod, I have to sing that? On video?"

"I think reality has just set in," I reported. I pulled out my phone and waggled it. "Oh, I hope I'm the one who gets to be behind the camera." As if the sudden exposure to the sun would cause it to light up, my cell chose that time to start ringing. Looking at the display, I groaned. "It's MCU. Damn.

No, don't stop walking. I can multi-task. Hello?"

"Mr. Anderson? It's Isabella Murphy."

"Yes, Isabella. What can I do for you?" Our friendly MCU representative hesitated on the phone, as if she had suddenly become shy. "Bella? Still with me?"

"I'm sorry, Mr. Anderson. I'm here. It's just that … I've been tasked with asking you something, and I'm not sure how you're going to react."

This bit of news brought me to a stop. Concerned, Jillian took my hand.

"Is everything all right?" she whispered.

"I think so. Bella? Just come right out and say it. What does MCU want you to ask me to do?"

I heard Bella sigh into the phone. "MCU has received word that you will be working with the New Orleans Police Department, in an attempt to solve the attack at the Expo. Is this true?"

Holy crap on a cracker. How did my publisher find out about this? It was, what, only decided a scant fifteen minutes ago. Someone at the police department must have forwarded the information to my publisher. As for the *why* of the matter, I honestly had no idea.

"As a matter of fact, it *is* true. Bella, it's my turn to ask you something. How did you know I agreed to help them out with this case?"

"I'm sorry, but I've been forbidden from saying," Bella said. "So, it's true. You'll be attempting to figure out who's responsible. We, that is to say, MCU would like to send along a videographer to document your progress. What do you think?"

There was no need to consider. "Absolutely not."

Apparently, it wasn't the answer my representative was expecting to hear.

"Oh, er, may I ask why not?"

"The last thing I need is to have someone shadowing us while we try to figure out what is going on, and who is responsible. It's no offense to you, Bella, but this is something that is literally not going to happen."

"Not even if you are paid a stipend on your next advance?"

"I don't need your stipends, nor do I need an advance on my next book. In fact, I haven't asked about advances in years. Why should I start now? Besides, Bella, there's no way the police are going to allow a video crew along while we're working this case. So, if you want to get angry with someone, it'll have to be them."

There was a silence on the phone. It was then that I realized that either Isabella had someone standing behind her, feeding her information on what to say, or else there was a third person on the line, and he was in secret communication with her. After a few more seconds had elapsed, I cleared my throat.

"Bella? Go ahead and put him on."

"I-I'm sorry?"

"I just realized you're talking to Richard. Put him through, please."

"Umm …"

"Zack? I'm here. Sorry about the cloak and dagger routine."

"Richard. What's going on? You of all people should know I'm not a fan of people breathing down my neck. Well, you can add to that list I'm not a fan of being bribed."

"Bribed? You haven't heard what we're willing to offer."

"Sure I have. Bella mentioned a stipend."

"A million dollars, Zack. We're willing to give you an advance of a cool million if you'll let this person document your involvement with this case."

"A million dollar advance on what?" I wanted to know. "I haven't even decided what my next title is going to be, let alone when I'm going to publish it."

"Ah, we're hoping it'd be based on your adventures there," Richard finally admitted.

"You want me to write a book about this particular case?"

"That's our hope, yes."

"No."

"We're talking a million dollars, Zack."

"No."

"Can I ask why?"

"I write fiction, Richard. This would land squarely in non-fiction, and that's not something I do."

"There's a first time for everything, Zack."

"I'm aware, but not for this. The answer is no."

"But, what if you were to ..."

"Richard!" I interrupted, raising my voice to get his attention. Jillian looked over at me and raised her eyebrows, her way of asking if everything was all right. Nodding, I gave her a reassuring smile. "I hate to be the downer here, but this is something that's not going to happen. You need to let it go, pal."

Upon hearing those three specific words, I heard both Jillian and Tori giggle. Grinning, I looked at my friend, but he wouldn't make eye contact. His gaze had dropped to the ground.

"Well, I'm terribly sorry to hear that. I was hoping you'd be open to the idea of something new and exciting."

I was fine with ending the phone call as it was, but as soon as my representative came back with that particular phrase, I realized I couldn't let it end that way.

"You do realize my contract with MCU is open-ended, right? You people do know that I can up and leave and take my entire catalog with me at a moment's notice? I make certain that particular language is in each and every contract I sign with you people."

"Now, now, Zack, there's no need to get defensive. I was just saying ..."

"Nuh-uh. You were insinuating that you were disappointed in my decision, and that it could have ramifications in the long run. Well, you're right. There will be ramifications if this particular subject is brought up again. Don't go there, Richard. I like you guys. I like what MCU has done for me. But, there are quite a few publishers out there. Perhaps I should call one of them?"

There was silence on the phone.

"Richard? Still with me?"

"I'm here, Zachary. You're right. There's no need to take any drastic action, on either of our parts. Let's just forget about it, okay?"

Smiling, I nodded. "Consider it forgotten. Listen, I have to tell you that I'm feeling a little anxious about going back to that expo tomorrow. Could we possibly move it to somewhere else?"

"They've already canceled the remaining two days," Richard informed me.

"Makes sense. Um, are you guys going to be doing anything else?"

"If we did, would you be interested?" Richard hopefully asked.

"Possibly. Let me know when you know, all right?"

"It's a deal. Thanks, Zack."

"What did they want?" Jillian asked.

"To send along some person to record everything we do while I'm on this case. Then, they wanted me to turn it into a book. Long story short, they've chalked it up to a bad idea."

I felt twin tugs on the leashes. At the same time, a faint melody could be heard. The first thing I thought of was the ragtime bands I used to hear at Disneyland. Glancing up, we saw that we were approaching some type of jazz pub. The doors were open, the music was enticing, and if we didn't have the dogs with us, I'm sure we would have ended up going inside.

Sherlock and Watson pulled us up to the threshold of the pub. Looking through the doors, I could see a small stage in the back left corner, a nearby baby grand piano, and a collection of small tables scattered here and there. Like most bars, the pub had an impressive collection of alcohol in a wide variety of bottle shapes and sizes.

Just inside the front door, I could see a menu stand. Behind it was a wall of Mardi Gras masks and beads. Turning, I started to walk away when I felt Sherlock snort with frustration and dig in his heels.

"What is it, boy? There's nothing in there for us. Let's keep going, okay?" Both dogs lowered themselves to the ground and stayed there. I handed my phone to Tori. "You're closest. Would you snap a few pictures? That might get these two moving again."

That did the trick. Back on the move again, we approached another bar, on the opposite side of the street. Figuring we were going to be pulled across, I looked for the nearest crosswalk, only to be surprised into silence as both dogs strolled by the establishment without so much as giving it a second glance. Wondering what could possibly be going through their little corgi brains, I glanced at the pub as we walked by. This one was newer, cleaner, and had more people entering and exiting, yet their Royal Canineships elected to ignore it.

Dogs.

Several hours later, the four of us were companionably walking along Bourbon Street in silence, presumably each of us lost in our own thoughts.

"Hey, I've been meaning to ask you," I said, as I turned to Vance, "what did you find out about that doll? Remember what Brittany said? She wanted to know where the pins were stuck. Did anyone know?"

Vance nodded. "As a matter of fact, yeah. Clearly the techs here know what to pay attention to. I certainly didn't notice." My friend pulled out his notebook. Seriously, did he have that thing permanently attached to his hip? Then again, I had my small notebook with me at all times, so I probably ought to let that one go. "Let's see. There were two sticking in the chest, one in left side, and one up near his left shoulder."

"The guy who died," I slowly began. "They said he died because something pierced his heart. Could, um, that be the reason why?"

"Don't go off the deep end," Vance cautioned. "It's just a fluke."

"Oh, yeah?" Tori countered. "Tell him the rest of it. Tell him what you found out about the chest wound."

"What about the chest wound?" I urged. "What is she talking about?"

Vance sighed, and then shot a dark look at his

wife. "Now, don't go reading too much into this, but the chest wound on our victim? It wasn't one, but *two* puncture wounds."

"Just like the doll," I breathed in amazement.

Vance groaned. "See? That's why I didn't want to tell you. I knew you'd think the doll was responsible for the guy's death."

"We are in New Orleans," I reminded my friend. "Voodoo is practiced here. Couldn't there be some truth to what that doll is telling us?"

"It's just a doll, pal," Vance told me. "That's all."

"Did the dead guy have wounds on his side and shoulder?" Jillian asked.

I snapped my fingers. "Oooh, good question, dear. Well, did he?"

Vance's smug smirk was back. "As a matter of fact, no, he did not."

I let out a dejected sigh. "Oh."

"You sound disappointed," Vance observed.

"No, not really. Still, the doll has two pins to the chest and our victim has two puncture marks on his chest? That can't be a coincidence."

"What do we know about the deceased?" Tori asked. "Did he have any enemies?"

Vance pulled out his cell and began swiping a finger along the screen. "The NOPD sent the file to me. I think I remember seeing something on the dead guy. Okay, here it is. Frank Keppler, 38, single, and lived in Metairie, wherever that is. I'm assuming it's nearby?"

I nodded. "It's still considered part of the New

Orleans metropolitan area. The area wasn't too nice the last time I was here, and I can only assume it hasn't gotten any better."

"What wasn't nice about it?" Jillian wanted to know.

"Crime rates. It's not a safe place to live."

We approached the intersection of Bourbon and St. Peter. I was getting ready to suggest we turn left, but ... you guessed it. The dogs perked up and tugged on their leashes. Again.

"Hold up, guys. The dogs are on to something. Looks like they want to check out that gift shop over there."

"Tricou Gifts?" Jillian asked, as we stopped under the white sign with the blue writing.

I shrugged. "There's gotta be something here that's got their attention."

Behind me, I could hear Tori and Vance having a hushed conversation.

"I absolutely love the architecture here," Tori was saying. "It certainly looks like those are apartments on the upper floors."

"They probably are," Vance mused. "They must have a fantastic view of Mardi Gras each year."

"We should all come for Mardi Gras one of these years," Jillian decided, overhearing Vance's remark.

"You do know what happens during those parties, don't you?" I warily asked. I pointed inside the gift shop we were standing in front of. "See all the beads in there? Do you know what people typically do with them?"

Jillian swatted my arm. "Of course I know what they're for. I've been to a Mardi Gras once. Michael and I rented a room a little west of here six or seven years ago."

Michael was Jillian's late husband. The poor fellow died from cancer a few years before I lost my wife to a car wreck.

"How do *you* know what they're for?" Jillian countered.

Helplessly, I looked at Vance, who held up his hands in mock defeat. "Don't look at me, pal. You're the one who kicked open that door."

"I, uh, have read about it?"

Jillian smiled and shook her head. "Sure you have. Anyway, I think we'd all have fun here. So, have you figured out what Sherlock and Watson are looking at?"

I looked down at the dogs. Both corgis were gazing up at a display rack that the owner of the store must have placed outside. I could see baseball caps, postcards, tee shirts, some frilly thing I couldn't identify, and a slew of other things. Seriously, I'm surprised the display didn't buckle under the weight.

"See anything?" Jillian asked.

"You tell me. Look at all that stuff. How am I supposed to figure out what they're looking at? Hold them up and see what they react to?"

"Just take a few pictures and be done with it," Vance said. "You know you're going to do it anyway. We can all try to figure out what they're up to at a later time."

"Someone needs their dinner," Tori decided. She patted the side of Vance's face. "Don't you worry, dear. We'll get you something to eat."

"Can you not say that like I'm a five-year-old?" Vance complained.

"Then don't sound like one," Tori returned. She looked at the two of us and grinned. "Fifteen years of marriage. I know when my hubby is getting a case of the hungry-grumblies."

Vance snorted with exasperation, looked at his wife, and then shrugged. "Guilty as charged."

I hurriedly snapped a few pictures of the display rack in front of Tricou Gifts and just like that, the dogs were off.

"I don't think I'll ever understand them," I grumbled, as we fell into step behind Vance and Tori.

"They have to be some of the smartest dogs I have ever encountered," Jillian admitted. "I do wonder if there will ever be a day that we can all figure out how to solve a case before they do."

I looked back at the colorful display of trinkets and merchandise. "Probably not."

We turned left at St. Peter Street and were on the eastern side of the street, heading south. Almost immediately, I spotted an establishment I really didn't feel like visiting. I could only hope the dogs felt the same way.

"Look, there's another one," Jillian said. "This

one is Reverend Zombie's House of Voodoo. What do you think? Want to go inside?"

I looked through the open door and saw bones, books, skulls, necklaces, plates, charms, and hats. I also saw the vast majority of the wall was crammed with ceremonial masks, with just about every emotion depicted in various styles. There was a display case, just inside the door, which looked like it contained bright, colorful decks of cards. The more I thought about it, the more I decided they were probably Tarot cards.

Tori reached for a pamphlet hanging on a rack just outside the door.

"It says if you ever wanted to learn how to conduct your own voodoo ceremony, this place needs to be on your list of things to see. Any takers?"

I looked down at the dogs. Sherlock had approached the door, lowered his head to sniff the ground, and sneezed. The little corgi swiped at his nose with his stumpy leg a few times before turning around to look at me.

"Awwwooooowooooowoooo."

"Those low howls are absolutely adorable," Jillian said, as she smiled at Sherlock. "What are you trying to tell us, pretty boy?"

"Probably that he doesn't want to go in there," I guessed. "Look, he's not pulling at his leash. Neither of them are. Watson? What do you think? Do you want to go inside?"

Both corgis sat, as if they were mesmerized at the wide variety of merchandise visible through the open doorway. Sherlock turned to look at me and howled again.

"Awwwwwooooooo."

My eyes widened and I had to stifle a laugh. "Sherlock, that has got to be the shortest howl I have ever heard. You're clearly trying to tell me something. Wish I knew what, pal. All right. I'll start taking pics. Look, I got the door, the racks, and the stuff we can see inside. Will that appease your Royal Highness?"

The answer to that was clearly in the affirmative, since both dogs walked off, as if the voodoo shop was now no longer worthy of their attention.

We finally found a place to stop and rest about a block later. Jillian located a coffee shop, which happened to serve fresh sandwiches as well. And, on top of that, they had a nice shaded patio where we could sit with the dogs. The waiter oooh'ed and aaah'ed over the corgis and brought them a bowl of water.

"Don't you feel just a little bit guilty?" Jillian asked, as soon as our order arrived.

"About what?" I asked, as I took a bite of my sandwich.

"Look at us. We're all eating healthy. That is, all but you."

I looked down at my order. One Monte Cristo sandwich, deep-fried and dusted with powdered sugar. On my plate were three small dishes of various preserves, in which I was supposed to dip my bites of sandwich. What can I say? I love this thing whenever I'm at the Blue Bayou in Disneyland. From what I can see, this sandwich looks just as good, if not better, and cost a fraction of the price.

"Don't be jealous. If you want a bite, then all you have to do is ask. I'd be more than happy to share with you."

Jillian stared at me and then dropped her gaze to my sandwich. After a few moments, a sheepish smile appeared on her face and she speared a piece of sandwich with her fork. I pointed at the tiny bowl of strawberry jam.

"Dunk a corner in that and then tell me you haven't died and gone to heaven."

My fiancée did as instructed. A huge smile spread across her face.

"Very well. Objection withdrawn. That is, without a doubt, the best Monte Cristo sandwich outside of Anaheim."

I clinked my glass of soda with hers. "That's my girl."

"What time is it?" Tori asked.

Jillian checked her watch. "Twenty minutes past five."

"It sure is getting busy out there," Tori continued. "Makes my feet ache just thinking about all those people walking by."

The amount of foot traffic on Bourbon Street was approaching what I called DLI, which stood for Disneyland Levels of Insanity. If I didn't know any better, then I'd say people were starting to line up for some type of Mardi Gras festivities.

However, Mardi Gras had already happened several months ago.

"Is anyone in a rush?" Vance asked. "I don't know about you three, but I'm thinking this is a pretty sweet spot to sit back and just people-watch."

"No arguments here," I said, as I hooked a nearby empty chair with my foot and slid it over so that I could put my feet up.

Tori set her glass of iced tea on the table and cleared her throat. "Jillian? Have you and Zack thought about getting married at Lentari Cellars? It's big enough for everyone, isn't it?"

"We've considered it," Jillian admitted. "However, I'm with Zachary. I wouldn't want that many people at one of our houses. With weddings comes craziness, and if something happens, I'd just as soon it happens someplace else."

"Well, I think anyone in Pomme Valley would be more than willing to accommodate the two of you," Tori said, drawing a nod from Vance. "Business, home, or whatever, I think all you need to do is ask. Your wedding is going to be the talk of Pomme Valley for years to come."

Jillian blushed. "Tori, please. It's just going to be a regular wedding."

"Tell them about the guest list," I chuckled.

"What about it?" Tori wanted to know.

"Welllllll," Jillian began, "there might be a few names on the list."

"Which, of course, means the entire town," I

teased, as I lifted Jillian's hand to give it a quick kiss.

"Silly man, it does not."

For the record, the word *large* wouldn't have come close to touching the tip of the iceberg our wedding was going to be. However, that's a story that hasn't quite happened yet.

Suddenly, the hand I had just been kissing dug into my own. Jillian gasped with alarm and sat up straight as a board in her chair.

"What is it?" I asked, growing alarmed.

Right on cue, both dogs started letting off warning woofs. Jillian pointed across the street.

"I saw him! I just saw the mystery man from the security footage!"

The four of us leapt to our feet.

"Where?" Vance demanded. His phone was out and he was furiously typing out a text message.

"I don't see him now. He could have been … there he is! Do you see him? He's behind that group of tourists. I think … I think he's wearing the same outfit from earlier. Why he'd be wearing the same freakin' thing, I can't say."

I spotted him moving purposefully through the crowd of people. He had to be at least two hundred feet away, and gaining. I caught a flash of the guy's hair. Yes, his hair was red, and they were dreadlocks!

"Follow him!" Vance cried, as he threw a fistful of bills on the cheque our waiter had just dropped off a few minutes ago.

"Call it in!" I said, as I hurriedly snatched up Sherlock and Watson's leashes. "We can't let him get away!"

FIVE

W e let him get away," I groaned, miserably, nearly thirty minutes later. "How is that even possible?"

"I'll tell you how it's possible," Vance began, and hooked a thumb at the sea of people filling the street. "There are just too many flippin' people out there."

I grinned and turned to my friend. "Flippin'? You watch your language, young man."

Vance gave me a sheepish smile. "I'm really trying to cut down on the profanity. Do you know how much money I've personally had to add to the swear jar in my house?"

Tori laughed. "It's a lot."

"On the verge of being able to buy their own brand-new phones," Vance grumbled.

"You have no one to blame but yourself," Tori scolded. "Besides, Vicki and Tiffany really appreciate your contributions."

"I'll bet they do," Vance pouted. "Oh, son of a … here comes Detective Martins …"

"And his shadow," I added, catching sight of his consultant, bringing up the rear.

"… and we have nothing good to tell them. That's just peachy."

"Detective Samuelson," Martins said, by way of greeting.

"Detective Martins," Vance returned.

"Our person-of-interest managed to slip away," Detective Martins glumly reported. "I have five patrolmen scouring the area, but so far, there have been no further sightings."

"I still say he's holed up somewhere," Vance said, looking back at the many shops lining St. Peter Street. "He's there, just biding his time. I swear it."

"For the record," the New Orleans detective said, "I believe you. But, until he surfaces again, we simply don't have the manpower to search each and every one of those addresses."

"I understand."

"If you see him again, you have my number," Detective Martins said. "Call me at any time."

"Will do. I appreciate it."

Once the detective was gone, Vance let out a groan. "Man, that ticks me off. I haven't lost a person in years. Years! Yet it happened, right under my nose."

"It's not your fault, pal," I pointed out. "Not even the dogs could follow him. There were just too many people out there."

"We'll find him again," Jillian assured him.

My cell phone chose that time to start ringing. It was a generic ring, which meant the caller wasn't among my list of contacts.

"Hello?"

"Mr. Anderson? Zack? It's Richard."

"Hey there, Richard. Dare I ask what's up? What can I do for you?"

"It's funny you should say it like that," Richard slowly began. "I, that is to say, we at MCU have a request for you."

I nodded. A request. That was much better than trying to have them believe they could order me around.

"What's on your mind?" I cheerfully inquired. But, I will also mention that it felt like my guard was now up.

"Have you ever heard of Charlie Goodman?"

"I can't say that I have, Richard. Who is he?"

"She, actually. It's short for Charlene. Anyway, Charlie Goodman is a very well-known New Orleans podcaster, with thousands of followers. She had a last-minute cancellation on her show for tonight, and once we told her you were available, she jumped at the chance to have you as a guest."

"A podcast," I repeated. "There's something I haven't considered in a while."

"You've been on one before?" Richard asked. "I'm surprised that I didn't know that."

"It was before I signed with MCU," I explained.

"It was years ago. I participated in a self-help for authors podcast. I really wasn't a fan of it."

"Would you be interested in doing this one?" Richard hopefully asked.

I briefly entertained the notion of turning him down, but then again, I don't think I have ever had a disagreement with MCU before. I didn't want any hard feelings, so, I suppose a little bit of appreciation couldn't hurt.

"Sure, I'll do it, Richard. Just tell me where it's being held, and what time I need to be there."

"Awesome! You rock, Zack! All right, do you have a pen? I'll give you the address."

Tucking the sheet of paper with the address into my pocket, I promised to be at Charlie's place at the duly-designated time. I just had to find out when her show was taking place.

"At six p.m. tonight."

"Uh, Richard?"

"Yes?"

"Did you happen to see what time it is now?"

"Yep. It's 3:45 p.m. That'll give you just over two hours to get there."

"Richard?"

"Yes?"

"You're in Los Angeles, isn't that right?"

"Yes. Why do you ask?"

"I'm currently in Louisiana. What time zone do you think it is here?"

"Oh, I don't know. Central?"

"Correct. So, what does that make the current

time?"

"Let's see, it would be … oh, no. It's nearly 5:45 pm! How the heck did I miss that? Well, shoot. I suppose we could …"

I flagged down the nearest taxi and showed the driver the address.

"How quickly can you get me there?"

A smiling black man glanced at the paper and nodded. "That's in the Garden district, uptown. It's about ten blocks away. I'll get you there in less than ten minutes, sir."

"Richard? Did you catch all that?"

"You bet I did. I owe you big, my friend."

"I wonder how long he's known about this podcast," Jillian quietly asked.

"MCU just now asked me to call," Richard said, overhearing Jillian's question.

"It's short notice," I admitted, "but we can make it." Richard forgot that I'm currently two hours ahead of him.

"Vance? Tori? Listen, we have to run. My publisher has set up a podcast I'm going to be on nearby. You guys shouldn't have to be subjected to that, so I'll do it on my own. Do you think you guys will be okay?"

Vance waved us off. "No worries, pal. We'll head back to the hotel. I was just thinking I'd like to go over my notes."

"At the pool, right?" Tori asked, raising an eyebrow. "You read your notes at the pool so I can go for a swim."

Thanking our friends, the two of us each grabbed a dog and hurried into the back of the waiting cab. Once we were on our way, I turned to Jillian and shook my head.

"I have no idea how long this is going to last. For all I know, it could be several hours. Are you sure you don't want to go back to the hotel?"

Jillian pulled out her phone and began tapping the screen. "Most book podcasts, my heavens, there are a lot of them, but as I was saying, most book podcasts are about an hour. That isn't bad. And this Charlie Goodman person? Her shows typically last forty-five minutes. Wow, she's everywhere. I think MCU did a fantastic job in setting this up."

"I'm here, right? Might as well get on MCU's good side, I suppose."

"You think you aren't?" Jillian asked. Her surprise was evident in her tone.

"Well, I've been kinda curt with them the last day or so. Then again, in my defense, I don't like to be surprised. It puts me on edge."

"You liked the last birthday party I threw for you. You had no idea what was going to happen when we walked into Casa de Joe's. And there you were, wearing that ridiculous birthday sombrero, while they all sang happy birthday to you."

"Family and friends are one thing," I told her, "but surprises from strangers are something else entirely. I was glad to see everyone there. But, to have hundreds of people staring at me? It's unnerving."

"I thought you handled yourself very well," Jillian praised, as she took my hand in hers.

"You heard how I deal with it, right?" I asked. "Eyes down, avoid eye contact, and maybe — just maybe — I won't pass out."

Jillian giggled and swatted me on the arm.

"Here we are," the driver announced. As promised, he deposited us at our destination right on time. "Y'all have a nice day now."

I thanked the driver, added a sizeable tip to the digital checkout on my phone, and turned to discover we were standing in the driveway of a raised center-hall cottage. I discovered later that these types of houses were essentially urban versions of French-Colonial plantations. The house was two-story, had pillars on both the lower and upper floors, and had wrap-around porches on both levels as well. This particular house was a medium gray color, with dark charcoal highlights and white wooden outlines around the windows and doors.

"Are you Zachary Anderson?" a female voice suddenly asked.

I turned to see a brown-haired girl in her mid-twenties standing perfectly still on the upper porch. She was wearing a long sleeved, light blue shirt and a white pair of overalls, only they ended above her knees. Round, wire-rimmed glasses were perched on her nose and her brown hair was pulled up in a ponytail.

"That's me," I confirmed. "Ms. Goodman?"

"Please, call me Charlie. Come on in. I'll meet you downstairs. Don't mind the mess. It's my housekeeper's year off, and I wasn't expecting guests."

Taking Jillian's hand, and making sure I had a good grip on the dogs' leashes, we stepped up, onto the porch. I was reaching for the doorbell when Jillian playfully slapped my hand away.

"You heard her. We're supposed to go on in."

"Do you usually waltz right into a stranger's house?" I asked, surprised.

"Of course not. But, in this case, we were invited."

We had only made it a few steps inside a *very* cluttered house, passing a kitchen with a sink full of stacked dirty dishes, when Charlie appeared in a doorway on the right.

"Come on up. We're about to get underway, so … wow! You have dogs with you! I didn't even notice!"

"Is that okay?" Jillian asked. "If not, it's all right. I can wait outside."

"Where are my manners?" I chuckled. "Ms. Goodman, er, Charlie, this is Jillian, my fiancée. Down there are Sherlock, with the black on his coat, and …"

"Watson!" Charlie cried. "Omigod, I don't believe it! Sherlock and Watson! You guys are from Oregon, aren't you? I love your dogs, Mr. Anderson!"

Taken aback, I looked at Jillian, who smiled and

shrugged.

"All right, I'll bite," I said, as I grinned at the girl. "How? How do you know these two? And please, if I have to call you Charlie, then you can call me Zack."

Charlie turned and disappeared through the doorway. We followed, and were surprised to see a flight of steps going up. I turned to look back at the door and whistled. From the ground floor, it looked like this door should lead into a normal bedroom. However, the only thing behind this particular door was a staircase. A common occurrence in this type of house? I guess it'd be cool if I thought of it like a hidden staircase.

"Welcome to my studio," Charlene announced, as we emerged onto the second floor.

Jillian and I came to a stop. The lower floor might have been a cluttered mess, but up here? Everything was pristine, organized, and meticulously clean. I saw a high-end computer tower, complete with a LED-enabled, specialized cooling case. There was a professional-looking microphone on a folding, moveable metal arm. Draped across it was a pair of over-the-ear headphones. At least three keyboards were splayed out next to each other, which made me wonder if there were several other computers present, only they were tucked away inside their respective desks.

And speaking of desks, the biggest, fanciest desk I have ever seen ran the entire length of the northern wall. Based on all the computer desks I've seen, this one had to be at least four times larger than anything on the market. I nudged Jillian and pointed at the monstrosity.

"Get a load of that. Now *that* is the desk for me."

"You don't have room in your house for a desk that size," Jillian pointed out.

"If you ever do want something this size," Charlene said, as she slipped behind the desk and took the only chair visible, "let me know. I had this one built especially for this house. I can give you the guy's number."

We were directed to pull out several folding chairs from a nearby closet. Then, Charlene handed each of us a set of wireless headphones. She caught sight of the clock on the wall, cursed, and quickly slipped her headphones over her ears. She then started tapping away on her computer. After a few moments, she smiled, swung the microphone around until it was in the desired position, and then began to talk.

"Good evening! This is Charlie Goodman, coming to you live from the Big Easy! Peeps, I have a treat for you today. I thought I was going to have to dig up some old book reviews, seeing how my scheduled guest ended up bowing out at the last minute, but instead, I'm very pleased to announce a special guest. Meet Zachary Anderson, author extraordinaire. He's the author of the current best seller *Heart of Éire*, currently sitting at the top of the charts at practically every online book seller you can think of. Before you start blowing up my phone lines, let me just add that he wrote the book under his pseudonym, Jim McGee. Now, this book has become a *USA Today* best seller, and as of last week, cracked into the coveted *New York Times* best seller list, too. Zack, welcome to the show."

"Thanks for having me," I returned. It was right about then that I noticed that, apart from the huge desk occupying a significant chunk of room in the upper floor, every *other* space was filled with bookcases. And, of course, those cases were filled to the absolute brim with books. "It's an honor to be here, Charlie."

"Are you enjoying your visit to New Orleans?"

"I'm quite sure I'll never forget it," I chuckled.

"And with Zack today is his lovely fiancée, Ms. Jillian Cooper. Jillian, what's it like to be engaged to such a talented guy as Zack?"

Jillian took my hand as I felt my face flame up. Swell.

"Oooh, good question. Well, I'd have to say that there's never a dull moment. Zack is the most kind, thoughtful man I think I have ever known. It was love at first sight."

"Aww, how sweet!" Charlie exclaimed, shooting the two of us a beaming smile. "Let's talk about *Heart of Éire*, shall we? I mean, I was lucky enough to receive an ARC copy, and I loved it the minute I first opened it up."

"ARC copy?" Jillian repeated, confused.

"Advanced reader copy," I translated. "My publisher will frequently send them out early in a bid to get those reviews in as soon as possible."

For the next twenty minutes, I regaled Charlie and her listeners with stories about how Vance's anniversary present came to be. I made Charlie laugh when I brought up Vance and his penchant for finding himself on the receiving end of jokes gone wrong, and I made her coo with delight, after I told her about Tori's first reaction once she realized what Vance had done for her.

"And you're sharing your sales with them?" Charlie asked.

"Yep. It was only fair. That book wouldn't have been written if it weren't for them."

"That's very generous of you," Charlie decided.

"It's just the type of guy he is," Jillian assured our host.

"Why don't we take a quick break, say five minutes or so, and then we'll go to the phones. Peeps? Back in just a few."

Charlie made a show of clicking her mouse. "And we're currently off. Well, what do you think so far?"

"It's no different from most interviews I've done," I decided.

"Can you tell how many people are currently listening to you?" Jillian asked.

Charlie leaned forward and typed several commands on her computer. "Just then? About two thousand."

"People?" I sputtered. "Seriously?"

"We'll get way more hits once the show is uploaded to Apple, Spotify, and so on."

"Impressive," I said, as I glanced around at the many bookcases. Everywhere I looked, there were books. "You've got quite a collection here."

"It's amazing what people will do for some publicity," Charlie said, shrugging. "But, I will say for the record, I have read each and every book you see. I only accept solicitations from authors whose books interest me."

"I'm glad mine did," I told her.

"I've been a fan of yours since *Misty Rains*," Charlie admitted.

"You knew Zachary wrote under another pen name!" Jillian exclaimed. "Good for you!"

"When you've read as many books as I have," Charlie explained, "you start to recognize similar writing styles. So, imagine my surprise when I started reading *Heart of Éire*, and I found myself comparing the flow of the story to several others I've read. That's when I realized Jim McGee's writing style matched up with another of my favorite authors. One who shall not be named, that is."

"Wow, I need to work on my anonymity," I laughed.

Charlie's phone beeped. She hurriedly slipped her headphones back on and tapped a few commands on her keyboard.

"And we're back, sitting here with Zachary Anderson, aka Jim McGee, author of the best-seller *Heart of Éire*. Zack? It looks like we have a few people waiting to talk to you. I ... all right, there's a few more. Peeps, you're awesome! Thank you for … wow, if everyone keeps calling at the same time, the wait time is gonna be horrendous. Take your time, people. We still have almost a half-hour. Now, first caller. State your name and your question."

"Hi, Charlie!" a high-pitched female voice suddenly said. "I've been a big fan of your podcast for several years now. This is the first time I've ever had the urge to call in."

"Thank you," Charlie said, as she waited for the caller to identify herself. When nothing else was said, Charlie rolled her eyes. "What's your name, caller?"

"Mandy."

Charlie looked at me with exasperation and shook her head. "Hello, Mandy. What's your question?"

"Mr. Anderson? It's so wonderful to meet you! I have a question for you."

"I was kinda hopin' you did," I returned, grinning as I did so.

"How can you write about a place so well that it feels like … like … well, like I'm actually there! How do you do it?"

"I would imagine it has something to do with the fact that I *was* actually there. If you get a chance, Mandy, I would encourage you to visit Ireland. Make it happen. I guarantee it'll take your breath away. It's truly a magical place."

"All right," Charlie announced, "we have another caller. You're on with Charlie Goodman and Zachary Anderson. Go ahead, caller."

On and on it went. At one point, Charlie scribbled something on a sheet of paper and slid it over to me. Jillian and I leaned close to see what it was.

Current # of listeners: 4,045.

Surprised, I looked up at Charlie. She nodded and looked at something else on her screen. A second note was hastily scribbled out.

Current call queue: 14.

We took another break, only this time, the moment Charlie went offline, she hastily grabbed her cell phone.

"Dana? It's Charlie. Listen, you mentioned before that you want to get some experience podcasting, didn't you? Great. Get over here. I need your help manning the phones. What? Who's with you? Oh. Are they familiar with a computer? Think she'd want to help? I'd be more than happy to … omigod. What? No, well, in the time it's taken to place this call, my queue has gone from just over a dozen to thirty plus. Yeah. Thanks, Dana. Hurry, 'kay?"

Dana, Charlie explained later, was her little sister. And whoever else Dana was talking about must have been a close friend, because within ten minutes, two teenagers were standing before us. Charlie hastily interrupted me, after answering the latest caller's question, saying she'd be right back, all without giving any explanation.

"Watch this screen here, click that there, and

you're talking to the caller," Charlie hastily explained. "After you put on that headset, that is. Now, tell them that they may, or may not, be able to get online with our guest, due to the volume of callers. In the event that they can't, get their question, and perhaps I could get Zack to read them all, one after the other. Got it? Great."

The next caller to be put through surprised all of us, especially me. I was kind of expecting an occasional question about the recently returned Irish jewels, but surprisingly, it didn't come up. What *did* come up were questions about what happened at the expo yesterday.

"Hello, caller, you're on the air with Charlie Goodman and Zachary Anderson. What's your question?"

"Hey, Zack," a male voice said, "this is Tom, from Covington. Listen, I've got a question."

"And I've got an answer," I returned, having long grown comfortable with this type of interview.

"What do you think was the motivation for yesterday's attack at the book convention?"

Surprised, I looked over at Charlie.

"That's not a question about a book, Tom," Charlie hastily interrupted. "I'm going to need you to …"

"It's not a specific book question, but it is a question about an expo about books," Tom hastily pointed out.

"It's okay, Charlie," I said, waving a dismissive

hand. "I can answer it. Tom? The official answer is, I don't know. I wish I did. They've been having a devil of a time trying to identify the person of interest, as well as figure out what his motive could be for attacking the expo."

"Next caller," Charlie quickly announced, looking over at Dana. The younger sister nodded and clicked the appropriate button. "You're on the air with Charlie and Zack. What's your question?"

"Hi, Zack," another male voice said. "Is it true they found a voodoo doll at the crime scene?"

"And we have another question about yesterday's attack," Charlie groaned.

"Yes, there was, and no, as far as I'm aware, it hasn't been taken seriously."

I heard a gasp of surprise. Looking over at Dana, I saw she was nervously nudging her sister and pointing at her terminal's screen. Charlie leaned close, saw whatever it was she was supposed to see, and jerked up straight in her chair. She looked over at me and scribbled a third note.

# of listeners has jumped to over 15,000.

# of callers is 200. Service maxed out.

"Okay, look, peeps," Charlie nervously began, "Mr. Anderson is here to talk about his career as an author. He's not here to answer questions about yesterday's attack. I ... what's that?"

Dana's friend, Krissi, the second teenager, had whispered something in Charlie's ear.

"It looks like we have a caller from Pomme Valley, Oregon," Charlie said, as she looked over at me.

"Would you care to take it?"

I shared a curious glance with Jillian. "Absolutely. Put them through."

"Caller, you're on the air. What's your name and what's your question?"

"I was just wondering if you've made any progress on the case," an unusually nasal voice wanted to know. I got the distinct impression whoever it was wanted to disguise their voice. "Any news?"

"Harry?"

"Who's Harry?" the voice wanted to know.

Now, I *know* I've heard that voice before. I've heard it fairly recently, telling me he was going to look for … formula. Baby formula! That's it. He was going to check for stolen baby formula. This was a Pomme Valley police officer!

"Ah, now I recognize the voice. Hello, Officer Jones. How are things in PV today?"

There was a gasp of surprise and the call quickly terminated.

"That was Officer Jones?" Jillian said.

"Who is Officer Jones?" Charlie asked. "And no, don't tell me he's an officer in your home town. That's a given. If my show is gonna get pre-empted by a police investigation, I might as well know the facts."

"Well," I began, "the short version is confirming what you know. I hail from Pomme Valley, and so does Officer Jones. For those who don't know, PV is down in the southwestern area of Oregon. As for the facts, well, the PV police chief and the New Orleans police chief seem to have a little wager going, and that phone call seemed to be an attempt to get some news."

"A wager?" Charlie repeated. A smile formed. "All right, you've piqued my curiosity. What's the wager?"

"That *they*," and I pointed straight down to the corgis, "will solve the case before the local New Orleans police does."

"Your dogs? Your dogs have been challenged to solve a case before the local police department?"

I smiled and nodded. "Sounds weird, but yeah, that's right."

Charlie leaned forward and fixed her brown eyes on me. "All right, Mr. Anderson. What am I missing? Why would the local cops challenge your dogs to solve an ongoing police investigation? Unless ... wait. You're telling me they've solved cases before?"

I nodded again. "Guilty as charged. If you'll pardon the pun, they're quite good at sniffing out clues."

"I see I'm going to have to dig into this a little bit more," Charlie admitted, giving the dogs a grin. Neither dog, I should mention, was looking at her. "So, about this wager. Do you know what the terms are?"

"I don't, no," I admitted.

"Are you, er, *they* winning?" Charlie asked. "Oh, for you people who are listening, I am talking about Zack's dogs. He has two corgis with him, aptly named Sherlock and Watson. And, it sounds like they've been challenged to solve the events from yesterday. That ought to make everyone happy."

Dana, who, like her sister, had on a pair of over-the-ear headphones, suddenly stiffened with surprise. She looked over at Charlie and I saw right away that her face was ashen. Charlie, unfortunately, didn't notice. Jillian did, though. Also at that time, both Jillian and I heard twin warning woofs. Glancing down at the floor, I saw that both corgis were awake, and both were staring directly at Dana. Coincidence?

"Er, excuse me, Charlie?" Jillian said, raising a hand. She then pointed it at Dana. "Is your sister all right?"

Charlie glanced at Jillian and then looked over at her sister. The look of alarm that spread over Charlie's face wasn't something I was going to be able to forget anytime soon.

"Guys? Stay where you are. I'll be right back."

Our podcaster quickly muted her microphone and paused her show. She turned to Dana.

"What's the matter? You're freakin' me out."

Dana turned to her computer and tapped the screen. "I think … I think you're gonna want to hear this one."

"Who is it?" Charlie asked, as she quickly rose out of her chair to see the caller's information on the screen. "The number is blocked. Hmm. There's no information. Have they identified themselves?"

Dana shook her head. She then looked over at me. "He says he wants to talk to your guest."

Charlie met my questioning look. "Zack? Are you okay taking this call? I've got a bad feeling about this. Something tells me that I shouldn't put this on the air."

"I'd still record it," I argued, growing nervous. Who could be on the call?

"Oh, there's no way I'm *not* recording it," Charlie stated, as she started typing commands on her computer. "Now, I'm not transmitting this, but I'm gonna make it sound like I am. Dana? Send him over."

Dana clicked her mouse and nodded affirmatively at us.

"Caller? You're on the air with Charlie Goodman and Zachary Anderson. What's your name and what's your question?"

"Who I am," an angry, distorted voice snapped, "is not important. As for my question, well, I won't ask it until you put us back on the air."

Charlie blinked a few times. "I'm sorry?"

"I know you're offline. Put me back online, now!"

"Perhaps when you have your own show you can call the shots," Charlie replied, growing angry. "But, until such time as that happens, I'm going to tell you that *I* dictate what will and will *not* happen here."

"If you don't want to learn more about the second attack," the distorted caller snarled, "then by all means, continue to feign stupidity. Otherwise, resume broadcasting."

It was Charlie's turn to turn pale.

"You ... you're the one who's responsible for yesterday's attack?"

"I am."

"How do we know you're not someone who's just looking for a little publicity?" I asked, growing angry.

"Like you?" the caller snapped. "As for me, I was wearing a black jacket and a yellow shirt. I know you found the doll and noticed Oya's veve. You were supposed to. How about I confirm the locations of the pins? One in the shoulder, two in the heart, and one on the side?"

"It's him," Jillian whispered. "The red-haired mystery man."

"Red-haired mystery man," the caller repeated, having overheard Jillian's comment. "I like that. Who else is on the line?"

"No one for you to be concerned about," I hastily snapped. "Now, will you drop all these theatrics? Just tell us what's on your mind."

"Very well, Mr. Author. I'll drop it for now. Now, *put this show back online.* I'm currently logged into your live feed, Ms. Goodman, so I'll know full well when it resumes."

Charlie looked at me, her eyes pleading with me to give her some advice. I nodded at her computer. Charlie held her breath and resumed her live show.

"A-all right, we're back," Charlie nervously began. "W-we have a caller on the phone who h-has a question for Mr. Anderson. G-go ahead, caller."

"Better," the male caller scowled. "Now, listen carefully, Mr. Anderson. I know you were at the book expo yesterday. I got to listen to you prattle on and on about your boring Irish drama, so now you're going to listen to me. Since I was interrupted before I could carry out my plans, I'm here to tell you all that there will be another attack."

Charlie gasped with alarm. Jillian covered her mouth in horror.

"Why?" I demanded. "Why would you do such a thing twice?"

"What's the matter, Anderson? You're the PV police consultant, you tell me? Haven't you or your two Dog Wonders figured it out yet?"

I looked down at the corgis, who by now, were sitting on their haunches and staring straight at me.

"How does a voodoo goddess fit into this?" I asked, hoping I could entice Mr. OffHisRocker to divulge a few tidbits. "What does Oya have to do with it?"

"No more answers, *writer*. Time is ticking. You'd best get moving."

The call abruptly terminated and we all heard a dial tone.

SIX

That was, without a doubt, the *best* show I've ever done! Holy cow! Can you believe it? I was talking to an actual wanted police suspect!"

"You make that sound like it's a good thing," I said, as Charlie led the way down the stairs.

"Man, you can't *buy* publicity like that!" Charlie continued. Her skin was flushed, her eyes were sparkling with energy, and she practically bounced down the steps. "Do you know how many people were tuned in before the police asked me to shut down? Go on. Guess!"

"Umm, I don't know. We do know it was jumping upwards. Maybe twenty thousand?"

"Try sixty-five!" Charlie all but cried out. "Sixty-five *thousand* people were tuned in to my show. That's more than three times my largest audience yet! Oh, I so need to thank MCU. Do you know if they like chocolates? I can send them a box.

Scratch that. I'll send 'em a case! Or, what about one of those fruit basket things? Oh, I know! How about something local? A gift basket with, I don't know, a variety of hot sauces? Maybe some gumbo?"

I laughed and held up my hands in an *I have no idea* gesture.

"How long before the police will let you air that episode?" Jillian asked.

"As soon as it is no longer an on-going investigation," Charlie answered. "That detective was very keen to point that out, along with all the fines and charges I'd be facing if I don't play by the rules. That's okay. I can wait. I am gonna promote the ever-lovin' crap outta this! Ohhh, I have so much to do."

Seeing the waiting taxi parked outside Charlie's house, I turned and held out my hand. "I'm sorry we didn't talk more about books."

Charlie batted my hand away and practically threw herself at me to encompass me in a hug. "Oh, no you don't. No apologies. Are you kidding me? You've given me such a boost in popularity that I have no idea how I'll ever repay you. In fact, I was really hoping I could get you back on the show once this case has been wrapped up and I'm actually allowed to talk about it. Oh, I'm sorry. I never told you. I actually did read *Heart of Éire*. I loved it!"

I laughed and gave the podcaster a friendly smile. "Thanks for that, Charlie. All right, you're on. I can't say when that'll be, but as soon as I'm able, then we should definitely think about trying a do-over. Did the police give any estimates how long they think it'll take before you'll be cleared to release this particular episode?"

Charlie shook her head. "No matter how much I pushed, I couldn't get a definitive answer. But, tell you what, there's the detective, right over there. He might know."

Glancing over, I groaned. It was Detective Martins, with his ever present shadow, Gregory Plinth. The two men had placed themselves between us and our cab and neither wore smiles. Looks like we weren't getting out of here without getting grilled. Again.

"Hello again, Detective Martins," I said, raising my voice so that Jillian knew what was waiting for us.

"Mr. Anderson. We just seem to continue bumping into each other. Why is that, do you think?"

I shrugged. "Small town?"

"New Orleans has a population of nearly 400,000," the detective told me. He shook his head. "Could it be that you always seem to attract trouble?"

Before I could stop myself, I felt a soft snort of amusement slip out. "You act as though you know me. Or have been speaking with a friend of mine. According to him, I'm the epitome of bad luck."

"I've checked into you, Mr. Anderson," Detective Martins informed me. "You have quite the colorful history in Pomme Valley."

I stared expectantly at the detective, as though I was waiting for him to ask a question. As it happens, in this case, that's exactly what I was doing. I got the sense he was baiting me, and until I figured out what his angle was, I was *not* going to bite.

"Nothing to say, Mr. Anderson?"

"I'm sorry, did you ask a question? It sounded like a statement to me."

Jillian hooked her arm through mine. "And to me, as well. Where are you going with this, Mr. Martins?"

"That's *Detective* Martins." Jillian was sternly corrected.

"If you want to be called one, then I suggest you start acting like one," my fiancée calmly told the detective, as she brushed by him and reached for the door of the taxi.

"We *have* been working the case," Gregory Plinth suddenly added. "We know that our mystery caller knows his way around a telephone system."

"What's that supposed to mean?" I asked.

"He bounced the call through Prague, then Berlin, then ..."

"That's enough," Detective Martins snapped, as if knowing that particular bit of information was going to give us the leg up on this investigation.

"Whoever it is," Greg continued, "he's been able to conceal his location from us, and not even our techs have been able to track him."

"Then, I would say you have your work cut out

for you, wouldn't you?" Jillian said, as she ducked into the cab and slid all the way over to the left.

Martins' face flamed up, whether with anger or shame, I didn't know. Either way, he quickly hooked his arm through his consultant's and hastily led him away.

"What do you think his deal is today?" I asked, as I stooped to look into the cab's back seat. "He was being friendly at first, but today? Methinks he be having a bad day, m'lady."

Jillian giggled and then nodded. "He's definitely grasping at straws. I can only assume it's because we're closer to figuring out who our mystery man is than they are."

"How do you figure?" I asked, as I gently picked each corgi up and placed them inside the cab. Once seated next to Sherlock, I ruffled his fur and gave the driver the address to our hotel. "Granted, they couldn't trace the phone call, but how does that translate to us knowing more than him?"

"Because," Jillian patiently explained, "we keep managing to dig up additional leads, whereas he, as far as I can tell, hasn't."

Back at the hotel, the two of us had every intention of watching a movie in the room, in an attempt to wind down from a busy day, but the two of us, er, make that the *four* of us, were asleep before the opening credits had finished rolling.

* * *

"Where are we off to?" Tori had asked, when we

met up the following day. "Do either of you have anything you want to see?"

"No plans here," I had reported, drawing a nod from Jillian. "Do you have something the two of you would like to do?"

And that was why the four of us, with two dogs leading the way, were strolling down Decatur Street; Jillian and I, hand in hand, with a dog leash in each free hand. We stopped at the intersection of Esplanade Avenue and were waiting for the signal to indicate it was safe to proceed across. I glanced down at the dogs and saw that they both had their tongues out, were wearing their trademark corgi smiles on their faces, and were having the times of their lives.

The opposing traffic came to a stop and the signal switched from an angry red hand to a white walking man. I turned to my detective friend and nudged his shoulder.

"So, where are we heading? You said you'd tell us later. Is this *later* enough for you?"

"Well, I figured since we are in New Orleans," Vance began, as we all headed out across the wide six-lane street, "and this is the birthplace of jazz music, that maybe we could stop by Frenchmen Street. There's supposed to be a lot of history on that street."

"Vance Samuelson, are you a fan of jazz music?" Jillian asked, surprised. "How is it that I never knew that about you?"

"It didn't start out that way," Tori said, as Jillian

and I followed Tori and her husband across the wide Esplanade Avenue. "At first, he couldn't stand it."

"It grows on you," Vance admitted, looking back at us with a sheepish smile on his face.

"And that's where we're headed now?" I inquired.

Vance raised an arm over his head by way of answering. Clutched in his hand was a tourist map of the area. Sensing an opportunity to tease my friend, I cleared my throat.

"Tori? I don't suppose you happen to know where you're going, do you? I think I trust you more than him when it comes to directions."

"Smart man," Tori giggled. "And, to set your mind at ease, I do."

"Hey, I'm going in the right direction," Vance complained. "You don't have to make me sound like *him*."

Everyone in our group knew that I alone possessed the worst sense of direction. However, I think that was starting to rub off on Vance, because he's now been lost several times. The first was in a corn maze, which he swore up and down he could solve. For the record, he couldn't, not even with the cheat sheet map he was given. The second time was in my home city of Phoenix, Arizona. Vance got so turned around while trying to get out of the airport that I was almost forced to take the keys from him. Thankfully, everything worked out in the end.

I felt Jillian's hand squeeze mine as we walked. Glancing over at her, I saw that she was nodding her head in our friends' direction. Seeing my querulous look, Jillian sighed.

"Zachary, have you let the two of them know about the plans your publisher made for tomorrow night?"

"I thought we were returning home tomorrow night?" Vance asked, confused.

"I told that to MCU last night," I began. "Bella called just as we made it back to the room. MCU said they wanted her to see about asking us to stay an additional night, seeing how they've reserved the huge conference room at our hotel. They want to try again for another book signing. I tried to tell them you guys are needed back home, and we weren't planning on making any appearances, but it turns out that a crazy number of hardcovers have been sold. Get this: readers have expressed interest in having the three of us sign the book."

Tori's head whipped around. "Me? They want me to sign your book, too?"

"What in the world for?" Vance asked.

"I wrote it," I began, as I ticked off the fingers of my leash-wrapped hand, "but you're the one who asked me to write it in the first place, pal. And finally, there's Tori, who's the inspiration behind your request in the first place. MCU said they have been receiving tons of requests from readers for all three of us to sign copies of *Heart of Éire*."

"Sounds like fun!" Tori said, instantly agreeing.

She caught sight of Vance's frown and immediately took his hand in her own. Vance wiggled his arm this way and that, in an attempt to prevent Tori from digging her nails into his flesh, but it didn't work. "Isn't that right, dear? You'd be thrilled to sign however many books are placed in your hands, wouldn't you?"

It might have been phrased like a question, but it sure didn't sound like Tori expected an answer.

"When does this happen?" Vance wanted to know.

"Tomorrow afternoon, at 1 p.m."

"We'll be there. Tor? We'll have to call my parents, and ..."

"It's already been handled," Jillian assured our friend. "I talked to them earlier."

"And work?" Vance pressed.

"Chief Nelson wants this case solved, remember?" I reminded my friend. "He was leaning toward giving you a couple of PTO days back, provided we can win this wager."

Vance whistled with appreciation. "I don't know how you pulled that one off, since the chief is stingy as a ... well, let's just say he doesn't like to give back paid time off. Sure, why not? It's the least we can do."

Both corgis suddenly looked up at Vance and continued to watch him for at least the next couple of minutes. I was actually beginning to think that this would be the first time since the beginning of written records that Vance Samuelson, detective extraordinaire, did *not* have doggie biscuits with him. However, before I could think the thought, two biscuits were produced and presented to the dogs.

"You're kidding," I laughed. "Where were you hiding that bag? And how did you know you were going to need them?"

Vance shrugged, and was prepared to answer, when we caught sight of the street sign on the next intersection over.

"Frenchmen Street. That's the one you're looking for, isn't it?"

"I may have some bad news for you, honey," Tori suddenly announced. "I've been doing some research online. It looks like most of these places have live music ..."

"How is that a bad thing?" Vance wanted to know. "That's what I'd like to hear."

"... in the evening," Tori finished.

Vance's face fell. "Oh. Well, maybe we can find a couple of street musicians, or maybe a corner band."

"I think that only happens in the movies," I said.

Tori pointed about a block up the street. "Hey, there's something that's on the map."

"What is it?" Vance asked, leaning around his wife to see for himself. "Igor's Checkpoint Charlie's? Seriously? What kind of a name is that? Any idea what it is?"

"Sounds like a bar," I mused.

Vance nodded. "Yeah, it does to me, too."

"Checkpoint Charlie's," Tori read aloud, "is a music club, founded by the late Igor Margan. Hmm, it says here that it openly classifies itself as a dive bar, has live concerts there, and ... get this ... is also part laundromat."

"No freakin' way," Vance exclaimed, as we stopped in front of the bar, just shy of Frenchmen Street. "Should we go in?"

I pointed down at the dogs. "If you'd like to go in for a little, feel free. We'll stay out here."

"It says here that it's a non-smoking establishment," Tori read, "but I can see from the pictures that there are still people in there who smoke."

"You sure you don't mind?" Vance hopefully asked.

I nodded. "Sure, go ahead, pal. There's a couple of benches right over there. We'll be fine."

Grateful to be off my feet, I lined my backside up with the bench and let myself fall unceremoniously into a sitting position. Probably not the smartest move, seeing how the benches were cast iron, but at that point, I didn't care. Concerned, Jillian sat beside me and took my hand.

"Zachary, are you all right?"

"Oh, sure, I'm fine. Just grateful to be off my feet. How are the dogs doing?"

We both leaned forward to see what Sherlock and Watson were doing, only we needn't have bothered. Both were stretched out near our feet and panting contentedly. Figuring the dogs might enjoy some water, I slipped my backpack off, retrieved the cheap plastic bowl I always add to their honest-to-goodness diaper bag, and emptied some water from one of the water bottles I had in pouches on either side of my pack.

They both took a drink, with Watson drinking a bit more than Sherlock. When the corgis were done, I capped the water (leaving the bowl out in case they wanted more) and leaned back to enjoy watching the many people walking past.

"I'm still in utter shock that you agreed to do a book signing," Jillian said.

"It's definitely not something I was planning on doing," I admitted, "but this time around, more than I would have been affected. The royalty checks that have been coming? I thought Vance was going to pass out when I handed him the first. By the third one, I could tell that his whole outlook on writers had changed. Whether good or bad, I haven't decided, but if doing some publicity for the book increases sales, which it typically does, then we all benefit."

"That is very sweet of you," Jillian decided.

"Vance said something similar. You know what? I'm glad."

"Do you think they'll ever be able to find our mystery man?" Jillian asked, after several minutes of a comfortable silence had passed. She held out a hand, encouraging me to pass her a bottle of water.

I looked down at the dogs. "If he's here, then those two should be able to find him."

"I was actually referring to the local police department," Jillian said, smiling. "But, they'll do, too."

Sherlock looked up at Jillian. My fiancée reached down to scratch behind his ears, which I'm pretty sure made Sherlock drool. Not to be left out, Watson whined and tried to nudge Sherlock out of the way. After both dogs had received a well-deserved scratching, they settled down to take a nap.

"I'm still rather surprised that our prime suspect had the gall to call in to Charlie's podcast," I said. "And ... how did he know I was there? I mean, he asked for me by name! I'm still trying to wrap my head around that."

"I've been wondering that, too," Jillian confessed. "That suggests he has some personal vendetta against you, but is that even possible? Are you aware of anyone who'd hold that much of a grudge against you?"

I looked at Jillian and grinned. "Really? Can't you think of anyone?"

"Oh, come on," Jillian giggled, as she swatted my arm. "You don't have to worry about Abigail any more, and Taylor? She's still in prison, and will continue to be for a very long time."

I should explain. After inheriting my winery, the family who thought they'd be inheriting it hasn't stopped blaming me for every problem they've got. If ever a family needed counseling, it was that one. What's really sad is that they are part of my extended family, seeing how they're distantly related to my late wife. But, is that a relationship I'm willing to pursue? Absolutely not.

"Besides," Jillian continued, "I'm talking about someone locally. Or at the very least, from somewhere around this area. Can you not think of anyone else?"

"Not a one, I'm sorry to say. Hey, I like to think I'm a likeable guy! No, no matter how much I try, I can't think of anyone who'd be willing to hurt others in the process, all in an attempt to get at me." After considering the question for an additional few seconds, I shook my head. "Granted, I can get a temper on me, especially if I feel threatened, or think someone I care about is threatened. But, seeing how I haven't really done any type of public appearance like this in, well, practically forever, I'd have to say no. MCU sprung this trip on me at the last minute, so I can't imagine my presence pulled someone out of the woodwork, so to speak."

Jillian retrieved her phone from her purse and began tapping the screen. Several minutes later, she triumphantly held it up.

"I've got the answer."

"To what?" I wanted to know.

"About how our mystery man knew you'd be at Charlie Goodman's podcast. Your MCU profile page has a calendar function on it. Someone had updated it to say you were going to be a guest that night."

"Ah. Figures. At least that mystery is solved."

Fifteen minutes later, Vance and Tori emerged from Checkpoint Charlie's. Vance was holding a large shopping bag, which from my vantage point, looked as though it was stuffed to the brim with purchases. However, the one thing that both Jillian and I noticed was that the two of them had smiles on their faces, which I thought was very becoming. Not only that, they were swinging their clasped hands back and forth, like love-struck teenagers.

"That's sweet," Jillian quietly whispered in my ear.

I squeezed her hand in response.

"That place is really cool," Vance said, as he and his wife arrived at our bench. I quickly scooted out of the way so Tori could take a seat. "You wouldn't believe how much history that place has."

"Whatcha got in there?" I inquired, pointing at the bag.

"I found some really cool things," Vance began. He started pulling various items out of the bag. "All kinds of stuff, but the real treasure is this."

A carefully wrapped package was produced. My friend eyed the package for a few moments before he started working on the string holding it together. Tori laid a hand over his.

"Perhaps we should wait until we're back at the hotel. You paid a lot for that, and they did a great job packaging it up."

"What is it?" Jillian asked.

"An autographed program from a 1948 jazz festival held in Nice, France," Vance proudly proclaimed. "It's been co-signed by so many jazz greats that I … I …"

"It was a lot of money," Tori told us, "but thanks to you, Zack, we were able to purchase it. In fact, I spent the last ten minutes trying to convince Vance to buy it. He said it was too much money."

"All right, I'll bite," I said. "Who's signed it? I don't think I really know of that many jazz legends."

Vance looked at me and gave me a sheepish grin. "Oh, yeah? Think hard. Anyone who has heard any type of jazz music has heard this guy, and he signed my program!"

Jillian laughed delightedly. "Louis Armstrong."

Vance reverently held the tightly wrapped package aloft. "You got it. This program, right here, is signed by the great Louis Armstrong himself. Isn't that cool?"

"I'm happy for you, pal," I told my friend, and I meant it. I held out my backpack. "Want to put that thing in here? There's no sense carrying it around if you don't have to."

Tori nodded and took my pack. "Thanks, Zack. Look, dear. This backpack is designed to hold a laptop. It has the perfect place to put your memento."

"Get anything else?" I asked, as I watched Tori carefully slide Vance's prized program into the laptop pouch inside my backpack.

"A few trinkets, and a couple of souvenirs," Vance told me. "But that? That's the Holy Grail. Dude, I owe you big for this."

"I didn't buy that," I argued. "That's all you, pal."

Vance turned and made a sweeping gesture with his arm. "No, Zack, for all of this. If it wasn't for you, then I never would have dreamed I'd drop ten grand on a signed program."

"Ten grand?" I repeated, amazed. "Damn. One of these days you're gonna have to show me that program of yours and tell me about everyone who has signed it."

Vance and I bumped fists. "You're on. Tori? Jillian? What's the matter?"

At that exact moment, I heard both dogs woof a warning. Had something spooked them? Looking around the crowded block, I could only shrug. I didn't have a clue what I should be looking at. But, since I know full well whenever we're working a case, I needed to pay attention to whatever catches the dogs' interest, I took out my cell and snapped some pictures as I slowly spun in place. There. That ought to make them happy.

"Awwwwwooooooo," Sherlock howled.

"Oooooooo," Watson agreed, adding her own low, but cute as heck, howl to her packmate's.

I held up my camera in front of them. "Look, guys. I took some pictures. That should make you happy, right?"

People who were in the process of passing stared at me as though I had sprouted a second head. I immediately pointed at the dogs.

"And you've never done something so ridiculous that it bears repeating?" I asked, with a mock-offended tone.

People burst out laughing as they continued on their way. I looked down at the dogs.

"Well? This had better be good."

"Oh, it is, Zachary," Jillian answered, using a low, soft voice. "Guys? Do you see him?"

"I do, indeed," Vance said, as he silently returned my backpack.

"Who do you see?" I quietly asked.

"Our mystery man is right over there!" Jillian excitedly told me, in a hushed tone. "Do you see that Chinese take-out place across the street?"

I shielded my eyes and looked for myself. "The Dragon's Den?"

"Apparently, our mystery man doesn't feel like cooking tonight," Vance observed. His phone was out and he was tapping out text messages just as fast as he could.

"Are you sure it's him?" I anxiously asked.

"Sherlock and Watson spotted him first," Jillian said. "They both jerked awake like someone had hit them with a cattle prod."

Tori pointed north. "We're pretty sure he was headed south, on Esplanade, when he ducked into that little restaurant."

"Did anyone make eye contact?" Vance wanted to know, as the four of us headed toward the tiny eatery.

The girls shook their heads no. Sherlock and Watson, I'd like to point out, had switched to their Clydesdale personas and were threatening to hurry me along, whether I wanted to or not. Wrapping their leashes securely around my hand, I reined them in and, when they finally turned back to give me a look commonly referred to as corgi stink eye, I waggled a finger.

"Easy, guys. If he's in there, we don't want to spook him."

"Agreed," Vance said.

"Maybe the guy is just hungry," I decided.

Vance gave me a condescending look. "Zack, he's responsible for poisoning dozens of people, plus putting a toe tag on one of them, remember? It was a premeditated attack, and Red, here, is our prime suspect. Don't forget that."

"Well, how do you want to handle this?" I cautiously asked, as we positioned ourselves by an empty table on the restaurant's patio. "Should one of us go in?"

"The only one who will go in will be the one who's presently armed," Vance responded, matter-of-factly.

This took me by surprise. "Wait, you brought your gun? On vacation?"

Vance looked back at me as he headed toward the restaurant's front door. "Does this look like we're still on vacation?"

Once Vance had disappeared into the Dragon's Den, Tori looked at me and shook her head.

"It's not his service revolver, but the smaller .38 he carries on his ankle. I tried to tell him he wouldn't need it, but to be fair, he does on this particular occasion."

"I'll give you that. Whoa, heads up! Vance is back. Hey, pal, what is it? You look pissed."

"He's not in there," Vance informed us, scowling. He handed me a To-Go menu. "I cased the place. It didn't take long, 'cause there's not a lot of room in there. Zack, he wasn't in there."

"Maybe he was an employee?" Jillian hopefully asked.

"I asked about that, too," Vance said. "All of the staff have been there since about noon, and no one has left the place since they got there. Too busy."

"All three of you saw him go in there," I said, looking at my three companions, who nodded. "And now he's gone? Could he have slipped out the back?"

"There isn't a back door to the place," Vance told me. "I checked."

"Maybe not for customers, but I'll bet they do for employees," I argued. "Is there a possibility he slipped through the back and out that door?"

"Let's go see if there *is* a back door," Jillian said.

Several minutes later, Vance was cursing like a sailor.

"How did I miss this?"

"What I want to know," Jillian began, as she threw another dark look Vance's way after another expletive was shouted to the heavens, "is how did our guy know to even use the back door in the first place? Wouldn't that suggest he knew he was being watched?"

Vance stopped ranting and stared at Jillian with disbelief.

"What?" my fiancée nervously asked. "It's a valid question, isn't it?"

Vance's face softened and he took several deep breaths. "Sorry. Yeah, Tor, I know. I owe the swear jar back home a bundle. Well, I can afford it now." Tori chuckled, but didn't say anything. Vance looked at Jillian. "You just asked the million dollar question. It sounds like we were set up."

I pointed at the dogs. "They don't seem too concerned. Sherlock? Watson? Mr. Red Hair managed to give us the slip. Again. Would either of you care to take up the challenge in whether or not he can be found?"

Sherlock shook his collar, looked at his packmate, and immediately veered left. There, just to the side of the discreet doorway leading into the back of the Dragon's Den was a large green dumpster with a heavy black plastic lid. Sherlock and Watson trotted over to the waste bin, looked back at me, and promptly sat.

Driven by curiosity, I gently propped the lid up to peer inside. A foul stench wafted out. Actually, I think the air shimmered, much like a heat wave. That's how badly it stunk. With watering eyes, I yanked my shirt over my nose and handed the leashes to Jillian. Looking inside, I quickly forgot about the noxious fumes.

"What is it?" Vance asked. "What'd you find?"

Sensing I had found something worthwhile, Jillian handed me a napkin, so that I couldn't contaminate my find. Holding the item firmly in my hand, I turned back to my friend. I held the item up, for everyone to see.

It was a latex mask.

"I think I know why he was able to give us the slip. Our mystery man has been wearing a mask this whole time!"

SEVEN

"A re you trying to see how many times I hear your name on a daily basis?" Detective Martins demanded, as he and his consultant exited their car. "What is it you think you've found?"

Vance turned to point at the Dragon's Den directly behind them. "Our friend, the red-haired mystery man, was spotted a little while ago, inside this restaurant."

Martins' eyes widened with disbelief. "You're kidding. And you four just happened to be outside?"

"We find it suspicious, too," Vance confirmed. "I know this sounds weird, but if I didn't know any better, then I'd say this punk was tailing us. He *wanted* us to spot him."

"Tell me you know which direction he went," Greg Plinth implored. "Tell me you and your team of forensic specialists …"

The consultant didn't make the gesture, but

I could easily picture him adding the air-quotes signs around the forensics specialists jab.

"... were able to tail him back to his secret lair."

"Enough, Greg," Martins snapped. "Samuelson? Do you have anything to back this up?"

Vance turned to point at the dumpster. "It's over there, on the lid."

Martins and Plinth wandered over to the dumpster. Snapping on latex gloves, Detective Martins gingerly lifted the latex mask and let out an exclamation of surprise.

"Our suspect was wearing a mask. That little miscreant has been playing us for fools."

"My sentiments exactly," Vance said.

"Did you see him drop this in there?" Greg asked.

Vance and I, and even Detective Martins, stared at the consultant as if he had just started talking in tongues and his head had twisted all the way around.

"He's ditched the mask," Martins said, growing angry, but thankfully much of that anger appeared directed at his companion. "I'd say he knew you four were out there, and that he wanted to make a clean getaway."

"Then, why ditch the mask?" Jillian asked. "Won't you guys be able to check it for DNA? Why would this person want to leave something like this behind?"

"Maybe he didn't have a choice," I suggested. "He had to have seen us out there. If so, he would have recognized Vance and would've seen him entering the restaurant. He knew he had to get out of there."

Detective Martins nodded. "We'll take the mask and see if we can get anything off of it. Prints or DNA, I really don't care. Anything would be helpful at this stage. So, what's next for you guys?"

I turned to look back at the restaurant. Appetizing smells were wafting my way, and I'm sure I was moments away from having my stomach growl at me.

"Hey, I'm thinking we're going to find someplace to have lunch."

Vance laughed and we bumped fists. "Glad I wasn't the only one thinking it."

"Do you guys like dogs?" Martins asked, as he softened his voice.

I looked down at the corgis and nodded. "Obviously."

It was the detective's turn to laugh. "No, not those, but *dogs*. Hot dogs. There's a fantastic little place just up the street. They've got a great selection to choose from."

I nodded. "Thanks, amigo. We'll take you up on that. If you get any hits on that mask, would you let us know?"

The consultant's face immediately frowned, which suggested he was all for withholding any information until the wager had been won. Martins, on the other hand, was nodding.

"I will. Oh, Mr. Anderson, there's one more

thing."

The four of us had just started moving in the direction we were told to go when, in unison, we all turned.

"Yes?"

"Stop calling us."

I gave him a two-fingered salute. "I'll do my best."

Ten minutes later, we were two blocks north. In front of us was a prime example of a two-story Creole townhouse. The building was painted a vibrant, tropical blue color, which included the second floor. From what I could tell, the structure was built using the brick-between-posts style common in Creole construction. The second story had a huge balcony encompassing the entire upper floor. Protecting the balcony was an ornate wrought-iron railing, which had iron support beams running down to the ground below every seven feet in order to help support the weight.

"That's the kind of balcony I'd love to have," I said, grinning. "Then again, that style might look rather weird back in Pomme Valley."

Jillian looked up at the second story and shook her head. "Gallery."

"Huh?"

"That, up there? It's a gallery, not a balcony."

"What's the difference?" Vance wanted to know.

"If there are support beams running down to the sidewalk below," Jillian explained, as she pointed at the closest one, "then that means the city can tax the building's owner, since the sidewalk belongs to the city. In this case, you can see that the gallery runs the entire length of the floor. It's quite common with these Creole-style buildings."

"Personally, I love it," I said. "Reminds me of Disneyland."

Tori nodded. "New Orleans Square. It's my favorite land there. This is clearly where Disney drew his inspiration."

Vance pointed at a couple of empty tables on the second floor. "Want to grab those? Tori and I will go order some food."

"Are we allowed up there?" I asked. "Don't forget about Sherlock and Watson."

"Oh. I'll ask." Vance ducked through the doorway. Moments later, he was back. "Yep, same rules as PV. As long as the dogs stay on the patio, or in this case the balcony …"

"Gallery," Jillian, Tori, and I interrupted.

"Whatever. As long as they stay on the gallery, then they'll be fine. The cashier said there's a spiral staircase right around the corner."

Once we had our food in front of us, and we put out another bowl of water for the dogs, the four of us clinked our bottles together.

"I can get used to this, pal," Vance said, after he took a drink from his beer.

"Good," I told my friend. "Just so you know, book royalties never stop. As long as the interest remains, and the books sell, we'll continue to get those royalty checks."

"I'm in the wrong line of work," Vance mumbled, more to himself than anyone. "Tor? Are you sure you don't want a bite?"

"That is disgusting," Tori returned. "I know full well you ordered an alligator dog. I'm not coming anywhere near you until you brush your teeth."

Vance hooked his foot through Tori's chair and pulled her close. "C'mere, baby. Show me some love!"

"Oh, ewww! Gross! You nasty man."

It might've sounded like Tori was upset, but she was giggling like a school-girl. Holding Jillian's hand tightly in my own, we sat there, on the gallery of this Creole building, enjoying the view, the food, and the companionship. No one said anything. No one needed to.

Once we were done with lunch, and after being assured by the waitress that we would be able to remain on the gallery just as long as we'd like, the subject of tomorrow's activities came up once again.

"So, whose idea was it to use our hotel's convention center to host another book signing?" Jillian asked. She took my hand. "Was it you, Zachary?"

"Believe it or not, it wasn't. I really don't want to face another group of people, but MCU has been dropping some serious money on promoting this book, so I feel like I should, at the very least, try to do my part."

"Are they going to bring in any of the other authors?" Tori wanted to know.

"I know the other MCU authors will be there. I don't know about any other publishing companies. As far as I'm aware, MCU is the only one doing this."

"Do you think there'll be another attack?" Jillian worriedly asked.

"I sincerely doubt it," Vance scoffed.

I shook my head. "Richard, at MCU, assures me that there'll be plenty of security there. I doubt very much that they'll put any of us at risk."

"Without the big-name authors," Vance began, "will there be enough people there to warrant hosting one of these signings?"

I stared at my friend with mock outrage. "Thanks a lot, pal."

"That's not what I mean. Oomph! Damn, Tori, that one hurt. Look, I'm not trying to be a jerk or anything, I was just curious."

"One thing I'll say about my publisher," I said, as I reached down to give the dogs a scratching, "is that they know what they're doing. If they organize this thing, then that means people will show up. We just have to play our part. And, if no one does show? Well, I'll bring a deck of cards."

Vance laughed. "You're on."

"Woof."

Surprised, I glanced down at Sherlock. He was on his feet and staring intently at the steady flow of traffic passing beneath our feet.

"What is it?" I asked the dog, leaning down to stroke the fur on his back. "Smell something good? Or do you still smell Vance's nasty ..."

"Hey!" Vance protested. "Don't knock it 'til you try it!"

After scanning the area and not finding anything which stood out, I pocketed my phone and sat back in my chair, reaching for my drink at the same time. That's when I heard a whine, followed by someone shaking their collar, which usually meant Sherlock.

Pausing with my cup halfway to my mouth, I leaned forward and noticed both dogs seemed to be staring at the same fixed point in space, down at street level. However, thanks to the throngs of people slowly passing under us, I couldn't tell what they were staring at.

"Their heads aren't moving," Jillian said, as she studied the dogs. "Everything down there *is*. I don't know. Can anyone tell what they're barking at?"

I started scanning the street when my eyes opened wide with surprise. There's no way. He wasn't that ballsy, was he?

"Oh, you're not gonna believe this."

Vance appeared at my side. "What? What's the matter? Do you see something?"

"Yep," I confirmed. "I don't want to point right at him, but I think you guys should know I believe Tweedledee is back."

"You're kidding," Vance scoffed. "He's a wanted

man. I don't think he'd be stupid enough to try tailing us again."

"There's a guy across the street," I whispered, even though the tables next to us were empty, "and he appears to be leaning against that trash can there. You should be able to spot him. Einstein is still wearing the exact same outfit. No, you're looking too far to the left. Umm, if I were to face him in that direction, he'd be at about 2:30."

Vance looked across the street and searched for public garbage cans. A few moments later, I heard my friend spit out a soft curse. There, next to a small specialty bookstore, Vance had spotted our shadow.

"I'll be a monkey's uncle. It sure looks like the same guy. I mean, he obviously had another mask on him, unless he's naturally red-headed with dreadlocks."

"Can you see tattoos on his neck?" Jillian wanted to know.

Vance nodded. "Yep. I'm no expert, but they look the same as they did the last time. Can anyone see his shirt?"

The girls casually glanced over. Jillian started nodding. "Oh, I see him now. Black jacket, black pants, and black boots. I can't quite tell what color his shirt is, I'm sorry."

After a few moments, our notorious friend shifted his weight from his left leg to his right, which just so happened to cause his jacket to flare open, as if a gust of wind had caught it.

"Yellow," Tori reported.

"The same shade as before," I recalled.

"He's staring straight at us," Jillian added. "He knows we're here, Zachary. Why does he keep following us? He has to know the police are out looking for him. Why did he come back?"

"He wants us to notice him," Vance softly murmured. "He wants us to know he's following us."

Our mystery man must have decided he had lingered long enough to make his point. Moments later, he had joined a large group of identically dressed tourists and headed back the way we had come.

"Time to go," Vance reported. "We are *not* losing him again."

"Why does he keep revealing himself to us?" Tori asked, as we hurried down the spiraled stairs.

"Maybe he just wants attention," I guessed. "Either way, I plan on asking him personally."

Back on solid ground, Vance and I placed the dogs on the ground and then the two of us hurried off, with Sherlock and Watson leading the way. The problem was, and I've experienced this before, when the corgis are in pursuit of someone, they obviously don't stop to consider whether or not the hapless human holding the other end of the leash would be able to squeeze through the same openings they could. What did that mean for me?

"Pardon me. Oh, I'm so sorry. Look out, coming through! I'm terribly sorry, ma'am. It's not me, I swear. It's *them*. Oh, man. How in the world did you get their leashes wrapped around your …? Never mind. I'll fix it. Sherlock? Watson? Slow the ever lovin' eff down, will you?"

I was ignored. Both corgis had reverted to their alter-egos, which were a pair of Clydesdales, and were forcefully yanking me along at almost a run. A quick check behind me verified that the rest of my group were keeping up, at a leisurely pace I might add. How? Well, that's easy. The dogs were pulling a rather large, dim-witted human along, and they were doing a very effective job of clearing a path. So, while I was dragged along, with as much finesse as an iron plow hitched to a team of oxen, my friends were able to navigate through the crowd of people with minimal trouble.

"That looked like fun," Vance told me, when we finally came to a stop fifteen minutes later. "How's your arm, pal?"

I switched leashes to my other hand and flexed my left arm. "Oh, I'll be feeling that tomorrow. Where are we? Does anyone know?"

"We're on Royal Street," Jillian reported. "St. Peter is just up there. If we go right, then we'd find Reverend Zombie's House of Voodoo. If we go left, then we'll find that coffee shop we found before."

"I vote coffee shop," Tori announced. "I could go for something to drink." She nudged her husband. "These pursuits are fun! You make them sound so dangerous all the time."

"That's because it usually *is*," Vance returned. "I don't see him anywhere. Zack, are you sure we're still following him?"

"Tell that to my team of horses," I remarked, pointing at the corgis. "They're still chomping at the bit, if you'll pardon the pun, to keep going. I can only assume our guy is up there, somewhere."

"There he is!" Jillian suddenly exclaimed. Glancing over, I could see her standing to the side, next to the art studio we were currently passing. "He's about forty feet ahead of us!"

Vance nodded and pulled out his cell. "Detective Martins? This is Vance Samuelson. Yeah, long time no chat. Listen, that idiot appeared again, almost immediately after we finished lunch at the hot dog place. He knows he's been seen, so he took off. Yes, we're sure it's him. He's wearing the exact same outfit from before. What's that? Yes, he's wearing another mask, and it looks like it's the same one from before, so he should be easy to spot. I don't know, he had a spare? What? Our location? Westbound, on Royal Street. Closest cross street would be St. Peter. Yes, I've personally seen our guy. It's the same guy from the security footage. I'd hurry, if I were you. Somehow, this little punk keeps managing to slip away. I'd rather not let him this time around. You, too? Glad to hear it."

"Well?" Tori prompted, as we approached St. Peter Street. "How soon before they get here?"

"Their station is close," Vance said. He held up a hand, signaling everyone to wait. "Okay, he's heading left. C'mon, let's go. Oh, will you look at that? I think he noticed we were following. He just ducked into that gift shop. Not this time, pal."

Vance hurried into the store, intent on following our suspect at all costs. However, there was a steady stream of tourists both coming and going. Vance was going to be hard-pressed to follow anyone in that place.

A few minutes later, we heard the first siren in the distance. Nodding, I could only hope that the guy was still in the store. Before I could ask if anyone could see Vance, Sherlock and Watson suddenly perked up and started barking.

"Knock it off, you two. We're here because of you. Vance is checking out that store because of you. What more can we do?"

Jillian tapped my shoulder. "Umm, Zachary? The dogs are no longer looking at the store. They want to keep heading down St. Peter."

Confused, I checked the street to see if our guy was there. He wasn't. There were, however, plenty of people still milling about. Some were headed south, and others north. The corgis, though, wanted to veer south, and they wanted to go *badly*. Then, it dawned on me what happened. Our suspect had to have ditched his mask again! That little twerp must've waltzed right by with none of us the wiser.

"We need to get Vance's attention, and we need to do it *now*!" I said, growing anxious.

"What is ..." Jillian started to ask.

I pointed at the direction the dogs wanted to go. "Our guy? He took off his mask. Yes, it'll fool us, but not the dogs. Sherlock and Watson must have picked up his scent. If we don't get going and do so, like, right now, then we're gonna lose him!"

Jillian pointed at the dogs. "Get them to bark, Zachary. That'll get Vance's attention."

I looked at the dogs. Was there something I could do to incite some frenzied barking? Most dog owners will back me up when I say that practically all dogs have some type of trigger they'll respond to. Granted, it's usually different for each dog. In my case, both of my corgis have always had a keen sense of protectiveness over me. All I had to do was appear threatened.

A big guy, with arms full of tattoos, wearing a gray tank top and black shorts, wandered by with what I'm figuring was his girlfriend. I stepped directly in his way and held up my hands.

"Hey, I'm terribly sorry to bother you. I need your help. This may sound weird, but I need you to rush at me, as though you were going to pound me into pulp. Will you do that?"

The guy stared at me with a blank expression on his face. "Huh? You want me to pound you into pulp?"

I pointed at the dogs and then at the nearby store. "My friend is in there, but there's too many damn people in there to successfully get his attention. I need to draw him out. Down there are my two dogs, and they're very protective over me. If it looks like I'm being attacked, then they'll bark like crazy."

"Ah. Well, I've been asked to do crazier things than this."

The big guy lunged forward, his hands out-stretched, as though he was going to throttle me. Sherlock chose that time to look back at me, no doubt wondering why we weren't following our suspect. A split second later, Sherlock threw himself directly in front of me and was throwing deep, guttural barks at the guy. Moments later, Watson joined in.

"Thanks, pal. Sherlock? Watson? It's okay. We just needed you to bark."

"What's going on?" Vance asked, appearing by my side.

I pointed southwest. "I think our guy is now maskless. Sherlock and Watson started woofing out here, and then both wanted to resume our pursuit."

"That cocky bastard is trying to ditch us again," Vance breathed. "Come on, Zack! What are you waiting for? We need to catch him!"

"We were waiting on you," I grumbled, under my breath. I gave the dogs some slack. "Let's go, guys! Find him!"

And we were off, like a shot. The rest of my companions fell into step behind me and within moments, were practically sprinting down the sidewalk. I heard the approach of several sirens, but I honestly couldn't risk a glance to check where they were. It'd be my luck that we'd run by a light pole or something, and one corgi would go left, while the other went right, and before I could react accordingly, there'd be a Zachary-shaped profile hammered into the metal bar.

Thankfully, the corgis behaved themselves and remembered there was a large, ungainly biped sounding like he was having an asthma attack attached to the other end of the leash. People hastily ducked out of the way, but that was mainly because both Sherlock and Watson were barking their fool heads off. Corgis may be small, and are arguably the most adorable of the herding dogs, but if you get them riled up, then they sound like they're ready to tear you limb from limb.

"Samuelson!" I heard a voice call out.

"I'm here, Detective Martins!"

"Tell me you're in pursuit of our suspect!"

"We are, only …"

"Only what?" I heard the detective ask, after Vance had trailed off.

"Only we don't know what he looks like. We know he's not currently wearing the mask, so what he looks like now is anyone's guess."

"How far ahead is he?" a second voice asked. I turned to see who it was, only it was a police officer I hadn't met before. "Any idea where he's going?"

"I don't know," Vance admitted. "Zack? Can you tell?"

I was about to tell him I hadn't a clue, but up ahead, sudden movement caught my attention. A small figure, wearing a light gray hoodie and black shorts, suddenly turned around, let out an exasperated cry, and then bolted. The dogs were, as expected, going crazy. They wanted to pursue!

"Vance! Did you see that? I saw him! I think he's young. He's wearing a gray sweatshirt, with the hood up, and black shorts. He just took off!"

"Are you sure?" Vance asked. "He wasn't wearing that before. Did he just so happen to have a change of clothes with him?"

I pointed at the dogs. "Tell you what, when you catch him, then you can ask him, all right?"

Vance shrugged. "Whatever. I trust your dogs. Martins? Did you catch that?"

"We saw him," Detective Martins confirmed. He and about four other officers hurried off. "We'll take it from here."

The New Orleans detective ran for the closest squad car, which conveniently enough, was pacing us on the street. The siren blared to life and the three police cars sped off.

"Think they'll catch him?" Tori asked.

"I sure hope so," I said, giving a heavy sigh. I looked down at the dogs and had to laugh. Sherlock and Watson were looking at me with such a disdainful expression on their face that it made me smile. "Look at those two. They must think the worst of me, since we're not pursuing our suspect. Sherlock? Watson? Someone else is going to do all the hard work, for a change."

Sherlock let out an exasperated huff and plopped his rear down.

"That confirms he was our guy," Vance said, as

he squatted next to the dogs to give them a biscuit. "They're not trying to get us to run anymore. What can you remember about him, Zack? What'd he look like?"

I shrugged helplessly. "He had his hood up, so I couldn't get a good look at his face. But, I can tell you that I think he's young, probably nothing more than a teenager. He was short and lean."

Vance motioned for us to step out of the line of traffic. Not finding room enough for our small group, he pointed across the street.

"Let's go over there. I see an empty table."

"What restaurant is that?" Tori asked.

I gently inhaled and shook my head. "I don't care. Whatever it is, it smells good."

"How are you still hungry?" Jillian asked. "We just had lunch less than an hour ago!"

"Hot dogs don't count," I chuckled. "And besides, calories don't count on vacation. What are you worried about? We've been doing nothing but walking everywhere for the past couple of days."

"I'm with him," Vance declared. "It smells fantastic."

We sat down at the table and pulled several menus from the holder built into the napkin dispenser.

"Gumbo Stop," I read from the menu. "I hear about gumbo all the time, especially here, in New Orleans. Jillian? Do you know what's in it?"

"Do you want me to answer that, or would you, perhaps, like to just try a bowl?"

"Would I like it?" I cautiously asked.

Jillian shrugged. "I'm not sure, Zachary. I personally don't think there's anything spicy or offensive in there. Then again, I'm pretty sure you haven't had some of these ingredients before."

"Hit me with your best," I challenged. "Name one."

"Andouille sausage."

My confident smile rapidly changed to a look of uncertainty. Every instinct I have at my disposal was screaming at me to not take a chance and to, instead, choose something more generic. However, here we were, in New Orleans, and sitting in the company of close friends. Why not? What's the worst that could happen?

"Is it imported from Ireland?"

Jillian laughed. "No."

"Okay, I'll do it. I'll give it a try."

Jillian's eyes widened with surprise. "I'm impressed. Vance? Tori? Would you like to try some gumbo from Gumbo Stop?"

Our waiter appeared and looked expectantly at us. He was tall, thin, and young. Then again, I suppose everyone younger than me was going to be *young*. Let's just say if I could easily be the kid's father, then the kid was young.

"Four bowls of gumbo," Vance told the teenager.

"Which kind?" the waiter asked.

Kind? I grabbed the menu and looked. Ah, there it was. Essentially, you had your choice of meat.

"Sausage for me," I told the kid. I pointed at the

menu and slid it over to Vance and Tori. "Pick your protein."

Vance nodded. "I'll try the chicken."

"Shrimp for me," Tori decided.

Jillian nodded and pointed at Tori. "I'll have the shrimp, too. Thanks."

"Anything to drink?" the waiter politely inquired.

Vance eyed me and gave me a smile. "Let's see if I can do this. Three iced teas and one large diet soda."

"Three teas and one soda," the waiter repeated, as he scribbled the order down on his pad.

"Three teas and one *diet* soda," Vance corrected. "You know what? If you've got a bucket, just fill it up and give him a straw. He'll be happy and you won't be running back and forth, filling up his glass every five minutes."

The waiter looked over at me and waited to see if I was going to contradict what Vance said.

"I'd say he's full of it," I began, "but everyone at this table knows that'd be a lie. So, guilty as charged."

"I can't serve you soda in a bucket," the waiter said, using a nervous tone.

"That was a joke," I assured the kid. "Just a regular soda, thank you."

"Diet soda," Jillian corrected, with a smile.

A basket of bread was placed on our table, and surprisingly, a bowl of water for the dogs. I smiled my thanks at our waiter, but when he turned to leave, I suddenly looked at Jillian. A girl had placed the bread on our table.

"Wasn't she a *he* earlier?"

"Different kids oftentimes have different responsibilities in restaurants," Jillian explained. "Her job is probably to make certain everyone who sits down here has a fresh bowl of bread in front of them."

Our gumbo arrived and I automatically leaned forward to see if I could determine what the base ingredients for this dish were. However, what I *could* see were various colors of different sized chunks. What those chunks were, I could only guess. Eyeing my soda, and then giving Jillian a grin, I took my first bite, er, spoonful, of gumbo.

From the way everyone was staring at me, dogs included, it was clear I don't try enough new things in my life. I could tell from Vance's hopeful expression that he wanted me to hate it, or make a scene. Tori and Jillian, thankfully, just had curious looks on their faces. Did I like it?

Yes, I did.

It's hard to describe which particular ingredient stood out the most. I saw large chunks of meat, so I can assume that was the Andouille sausage Jillian mentioned. I could tell there were bell peppers floating in my bowl, and based on the color, I'd say red and green. Not originally a fan of peppers, these tasted just like everything else. Plus, I could tell that there were various other vegetables present, ranging from celery to onions, but again, everything tasted the same. With that being said, I just couldn't determine *what* that taste was.

Something large and green floated to the surface. Green pepper, it was *not*.

Now, let me pause here and say that, since becoming an adult, there are a few things that I absolutely refuse to eat. Yes, Jillian would probably have a few things to add, but in the top three would be green beans. I could never stomach them as a kid.

The thing floating in my bowl looked just like a green bean. Now, I'm sitting with my fiancée, and across the table from us were our good friends. The last thing I wanted to do was create a scene, especially when that was exactly what Vance was hoping I'd do. But, the sight of a green bean—childish, I know—was enough to bring me to an immediate stop.

Knowing full well how much I loathed the aforementioned veggie, Jillian saw me hesitate as I stared at my bowl. She leaned over my shoulder to see for herself what I was looking at.

"Okra," Jillian whispered in my ear. "It's not a green bean, nor is it a relative of one. Trust me, you're fine."

Steeling myself, I spooned it up and, with my hand casually holding onto my glass of soda, I gave it a try. As I mentioned with the other various bits and pieces in the gumbo, it all tasted the same. Relaxing somewhat, I finished my lunch. Or dinner. Hmm, I honestly didn't know what time it was.

"Do you like it?" Jillian asked.

I nodded. "It surprises me to say this, but yeah, I do."

I heard a soft snort from the ground. Looking down at the dogs, I could see Sherlock looking at me, but he had a look of derision on his face. You wouldn't think a dog could pull that off, but this corgi certainly could. I looked back at my bowl, then back at the dogs. I flashed back to all the restaurants we'd passed, and those businesses that had pulled the dogs to a stop. A notion occurred. Could I, just this once, have managed to fire up enough brain cells to figure this out before my two dogs could?

EIGHT

I'll save you the trouble. No, I hadn't. I thought I had, but as you'll soon see, I'm frequently wrong.

Pulling out my phone, I brought up the pictures I had taken on this trip and started going through them. Jillian noticed what I was doing and scooted her chair close.

"Oooh, are you going to look at corgi clues?"

Jillian asked that question just as the girl who kept refilling our breadbasket wandered by. The teenager looked at us, and then down at the dogs. A giggle escaped her lips.

"Corgi clues? Did I hear that right?"

I pointed at the dogs. "Long story short, Sherlock and Watson are able to …"

"Sherlock and Watson?" the girl interrupted, giggling again. "Those are their names?"

Upon hearing their names uttered by a stranger, both corgis looked up. Sherlock was on his feet first. Within moments, both dogs were pulling on their leashes in an effort to be the first one to receive adoration from their newest admirer.

"They are so cute!" the girl exclaimed. "They're named after those famous detectives?"

"That's one way of looking at it," I said, returning the teenager's smile.

"Too bad they don't hunt for clues. Wait. You said corgi clues. They don't, do they?"

Looking up, I shrugged. "What, find clues? Actually, they do. They are very proficient crime solvers."

"These dogs are police consultants in Oregon," Vance proudly announced. He showed the girl his badge. "I'm Detective Vance Samuelson. Zack and the dogs have helped on a number of cases. So, you heard right. They have found clues, only we haven't really figured them out yet."

I swiped at my phone a few times and showed the girl the picture my phone was now displaying.

"Do you see this one? Let's see. Looks like we have a menu. The dogs stopped at Café Beignet, if memory serves, and ... yep, got it right. You can see the restaurant's name up at the top left. Anyway, they expressed interest in looking at the menu. So, as soon as I took the picture, they settled down." I pointed at my phone and decided an explanation was necessary. "It means there's something in this picture they wanted me to see."

The girl leaned forward, nearly looking over my shoulder, to get a closer look at the picture.

"Café Beignet. I've been there many times. Their beignets are to die for!"

"How long have you lived in New Orleans?" Jillian asked, as she turned to look up at the girl. I watched my fiancée drop her gaze to the girl's uniform. "Aimee. That's a pretty name. Listen Aimee, do you think you can help us? We have some pictures here, and we might need some help identifying what we're looking at."

"Are you working a case right now?" the girl asked, her eyes widening with surprise.

"We are," I confirmed.

"And you're asking me for help?"

"Is that okay?" Vance asked.

The girl looked up and raised her voice. "Tomas? I'm taking my break, okay?"

We heard some faint shouting, coming from somewhere inside the restaurant. The girl smiled again and hastily pulled a chair from the adjacent table over to ours. That was when I got my first good look at the girl. Gumbo Stop's bread filler-upper had pale skin, jet black hair, and full eyebrows. Her face dimpled when she smiled, and so far, every time I've seen her, she's been smiling. In fact, she looked an awful lot like a young Jennifer Connelly.

"So, how can I help?"

"Let's start with a few introductions. You know those two are Sherlock and Watson. I'm Zack, this is Jillian, and over there are our good friends, Vance and Tori."

The girl's smile widened even further as she waved at everyone. "I'm Aimee. Aimee Chapman."

"What I'm going to do, Aimee," I began, "is show everyone the pictures Sherlock and Watson wanted me to take. Go on, laugh if you'd like. It wouldn't be the first time. At this table, you're the odd man out, so to speak, in that everyone here believes me when I say the dogs wanted these specific pictures taken."

"Amazing," Aimee breathed.

"Now, first off, we have …"

"Oya!" Aimee exclaimed, looking at the bizarre mark from our mystery man's neck. "You're telling me your dogs wanted you to take a picture of a veve? How do they even know what it is?"

"How do you?" I challenged. "For the record, yes, we had someone at a voodoo shop explain this mark to us. The person we're looking for had this tattooed on his neck."

"Of course I know what this is," Aimee insisted. "You can't live in New Orleans and not be familiar with veves. I should know. I'm a doctor."

Everyone at our table, excluding Aimee herself, suddenly sat back in their chairs and stared at the girl, as though she had become possessed. I'm sure all four of us had the same expression on our face: skepticism. I crossed my arms over my chest and waited for an explanation.

"You're a voodoo doctor?" Vance slowly asked, not bothering to hide his skepticism.

"Okay, okay, I may not be a *doctor*," Aimee

amended, "but I *am* a worker."

"I think you might need to clarify what you mean," Jillian told the girl.

"Doctors and workers are specialists in voodoo," Aimee explained. I got the feeling she has had to explain herself on more than one occasion. "It's a term used to describe someone who provides powders, perfumes, gris-gris, and even oils to clients. I haven't been practicing long, since I just learned my great-great-grandmother was a voodoo queen at the turn of the century. As you can imagine, it didn't go over too well with my parents when I told them I wanted to learn."

"I'll bet," Vance agreed. "Let me ask you, what do you think of it so far?"

"Of voodoo?" Aimee asked. "It's fascinating. There are so many things to learn if I truly want to provide a service to the people, like my ancestors did."

I tapped my phone's screen. "Well, I can say I'm impressed you were able to identify this particular mark."

Aimee blushed accordingly.

"What's next?" Jillian asked.

I swiped my finger to the right. "Oh, okay. Gang? Here's the voodoo doll that our suspect dropped at the convention center."

"The convention center?" Aimee repeated, losing her smile for the first time. "As in, the book expo that was going on this weekend?"

I nodded. "The one and the same. All of us were

there. Jillian and the dogs were in the audience, while Vance, Tori, and I were up at the panelist's table."

"You were presenting something? You're an author? I thought you said you were a police consultant?"

"He's both," Vance announced. I was surprised. I think that's one of the few times I've heard my detective friend come to my defense with regard to being an author. Usually, I'm teased about being a romance writer. "His book is currently on the *New York Times* best sellers list. Tori and I were up there 'cause I'm the one who persuaded Zack to write a book featuring my wife."

"*Heart of Éire*," Jillian answered, before Aimee could ask the inevitable question. "Perhaps you've heard of it?"

Aimee squealed with excitement and then pulled out her phone. "Heard of it? I'm currently reading it! You? You're Jim McGee? I thought it was Zachary Anderson?"

"It's one of the pseudonyms I've used," I admitted.

Suddenly, Aimee was leaning close and holding out her phone for a selfie. Realizing she was now invading my personal space, she blushed again before turning to look at Jillian.

"Do you mind if I get a picture with him?"

Jillian smiled and shook her head. Then, she held out a hand. "I'll take the picture, if you'd like."

Once our new friend's excitement had returned

to previous levels, we moved to the next picture.

"Café Beignet," Aimee observed. "Great place, awesome beignets."

"Couldn't agree more," I told her.

"What were the dogs looking at?" Tori wanted to know. "What's in the picture?"

I slid my phone over to the Samuelsons, who both leaned over to take a look.

"It's the menu," Vance answered. "Why? What's wrong with it?"

"I don't think there's anything wrong with it," I pointed out. "The resolution is good enough to zoom in and see what was on it. As far as I can tell, it's just a menu."

Jillian's turn with my phone was next. She studied the image for a few minutes before handing it to Aimee.

"I can't see anything that stands out, either."

"See anything?" I asked our new friend.

The phone was pushed back toward me. "No, I'm sorry."

"All-righty then. On to the next. Nope, it's another picture of the same menu. Moving on. Okay, here we go. Here's something I didn't take a picture of. Tori, I think this might have been you."

Tori blinked with surprise. "Me? Let me see. Oh, that's right. This was before Vance purchased his autographed program, when you handed me the phone to take a few pictures."

The phone was passed around the table. "Does anyone see anything in common?"

"Well, there's a menu visible," Jillian reported, "but no close-ups of it. I can only assume that whatever the dogs wanted us to see, it isn't on this particular menu."

"What can you see?" I asked, turning to our new friend.

The phone made its way into Aimee's hand. "Well, I see beads, trinkets, and all kinds of tourist stuff."

The phone was pushed toward me, but I ended up pushing it back. "There's three or four pictures there. Once these pictures were taken, the dogs settled down. Take a look at all of them, okay?"

Aimee nodded and swiped through the pictures. Studying each one intently, she sadly shook her head.

"There's nothing here any local would want. I'm sorry, it's all just junk."

"Nothing that any local would want," I repeated. "Could that be the key?" I backtracked a bit and looked at some of the previous pictures. "It's so darn difficult to figure out what we should be looking for. This pub had just about everything in it, so it … oh, look. The next three pictures are from that gift shop we passed."

"Which one?" Aimee asked. "I swear I've been to them all."

I swiped my phone's display a few times. "Hang on, I'm looking for a business name, or a sign, or …" I trailed off as I spotted Aimee's outstretched hand. "Fine. You look."

The girl took my phone and studied the picture. "Tricou Gifts."

"How do you know for sure?" Jillian wanted to know.

Aimee adjusted the image, so that the picture was zoomed in on the lower left corner. "Do you see these beads? The yellow and pink ones? Well, even though you can't see it, there's a tiny letter 'T' on the yellow beads and a 'G' on the pink ones. You can only get them there."

"Tricou Gifts," I repeated, nodding. "Okey dokey. What else can you tell from the pictures? Anything else stand out?"

"It's just more tourist stuff," Aimee decided, after a few minutes had passed in silence. "Hmm. Let me check something."

I watched the girl backtrack a few pictures. Then, she was nodding. Had she noticed something?

"Masks. Your dogs would appear to have a mask fetish. A lot of these pictures have some type of mask in the background."

Jillian nodded. "Well, that makes sense. We know our mystery man was wearing a mask when he pulled off his stunt at the expo."

I reclaimed my phone to look at the last set of pictures. They were of Checkpoint Charlie's, where Vance had dropped some serious money for an autographed music program. As I sat there, trying to think why I was looking at several pictures of the pub, Jillian leaned over and looked at the display.

"Checkpoint Charlie's. I remember this one. Sherlock and Watson woofed at you until some pictures were taken."

"Was this before or after Vance came out?" I wanted to know.

"After," Vance said, overhearing the question. "I remember hearing the dogs make some noise."

I zoomed in on the photo as much as I could and slowly panned it around. The problem was, there wasn't anything that stood out. I moved to the next picture, and then the next. As far as I could tell, they were all the same shot.

"Want a second opinion?" Aimee asked, upon hearing my dismayed groan.

Wordlessly, I slid the phone over to her. She studied the screen for several minutes before conceding defeat. That's when Jillian held out her hand. Without waiting for my permission, our young friend handed my phone to Jillian and then sat back in her chair, as though the very effort of looking at pictures exhausted her. That's when I noticed Jillian quickly sitting up in her chair. Her fingers danced over my phone's display as she hastily flipped between pictures. Glancing down at her hands, I could see the only pictures she was interested in were the ones taken at Checkpoint Charlie's.

"Did you find something?" I asked.

Jillian nodded excitedly. "Zachary, look here. This is the first picture you took. You can see people at the counter, and some squatting at this display case there."

Vance stood, leaned over the table, and nodded. "That's the case that had my program."

I nodded. "All right. With you so far."

"Zachary, look at this person right here," Jillian instructed, tapping a finger on a person visible in the distance. "Do you see him, next to that row of washers?"

"I forgot it's part laundromat," I chuckled. "Okay, yeah, I see him. What about him? He's too blurry to make anything out."

Jillian brought up the next image. "And this one? The same guy is a literal blur of motion as he ducks behind that rack."

Unsure where Jillian was going with this line of questioning, I smiled and nodded.

"And finally," Jillian continued, as she brought up the third and final picture taken inside Checkpoint Charlie's, "you see the guy rapidly heading for the door."

"His head is down," I reported. "We have no idea who this guy is."

Jillian zoomed in on the guy's right hand. "Do you see what he's holding?"

I squinted at the picture. "Something is rolled up in his hand, but I can't make out what."

"Who has the best eyes?" Jillian asked, as she looked around our table. "I need someone to verify what I see here."

"What do you see?" Tori wanted to know. "Here,

give it to me. My eyes are pretty good. This? This person here? Okay, I see what you're talking about. It looks like … Jillian? Is that a red dreadlock sticking out from the rolled up whatever-it-is? Is this our mystery man, holding his rolled-up mask?"

Jillian nodded excitedly. "That's precisely what I think we're looking at. Somehow, the dogs knew our mystery man was in there, watching us. I have a question. Can you make out any tattoos on the guy's neck?"

Tori squinted at the picture. "I can't tell. He has his hood up, which takes care of being able to see his neck. Why do you ask? Oh, I get it! You think the tattoos are just part of the mask?"

Jillian nodded. "I do, yes."

"What I want to know is," Vance began, "how does he even know who I am?"

"Because," I answered, "you were up there with me at the panel. He saw me up there, so it goes without saying that he saw you, too."

The table fell silent as my phone changed hands multiple times.

"I just wish we could see his face," Vance groaned, after he passed my phone to Tori. "It must've been dark back there."

"Auto-focus," Jillian reported. "The phone's camera was focused on the people in the foreground. Therefore, anything in the background would slip out of focus."

"Photos of menus," I began, "photos of trinkets and masks, and we're pretty sure we have pictures of our mystery man, only it's too blurry to make out. The masks I can understand, but I'm having trouble with the food element. Take Café Beignet. Aimee, you said you've been there before, right?"

"It's the best and only place to get fresh beignets," Aimee confirmed.

"What else do they have on the menu besides beignets?" Jillian asked.

Aimee shrugged. "Just about everything, I suppose. There are breakfast items, like omelets, sandwiches, drinks, and so on."

"Just like the rest of the menus," I sighed. "That doesn't really help us too much."

"It was a good idea," Vance told me.

"What's with you?" I demanded, as I looked at my friend. "Since when are you so nice and supportive?"

Vance pointed at my backpack. "Since you're still carrying my souvenir."

I laughed. "Good answer, pal. What do you guys think? Is it right to assume that, excluding the food pictures, we've got these figured out?"

"Since we haven't figured them out," Tori began, "then I can say it's safe to say they're probably the most important aspect of the investigation."

Our entire table fell silent as we each considered how the menu pictures fit into what we knew was going on. After a few moments, I ended up shrugging.

"Whatever the link is, it escapes me at this moment. Anyone have anything?"

There was a collective shaking of heads.

"I can see why you'd think that," Aimee agreed, as she leaned back in her chair. She caught sight of my full water glass and pointed at it. "May I?"

Nodding, I pushed the glass over to her. "Be my guest."

Taking a long drink from the glass, Aimee was silent for a few moments as she considered what she had seen.

"I think another link you might want to consider could be Mardi Gras."

Vance nodded. "I was thinking that, too. I've seen quite a few pictures with beads and masks, although, as mentioned earlier, the mask link isn't that difficult. Our mystery man was clearly wearing one when we were tailing him and vice-versa. It just means he's probably not a red-haired man."

Remembering something I had picked up as we were walking on Bourbon Street, I pulled my bag up to my lap and started searching through the various pockets. Finding what I was looking for, I stacked my empty bowl inside Jillian's, and then moved it and a few other dishes to a nearby unoccupied table in an attempt to make some room.

"Grab those salt and pepper shakers," I ordered, as I unfolded my tourist map. "All right, who has a pen?"

Jillian held up a purple felt-tip pen and waggled it in front of me. "Will this do?"

"Yes, it's perfect. Thanks. Okay, let's do this. I

want to mark the map everywhere Sherlock and Watson had us stop. Maybe it'll shed some light for us. So, first up, we have the convention center."

Jillian tapped a big rectangle on the map. "That would be here."

I passed her the pen. "Great. Circle it, would you?"

"What was next?" Tori wanted to know.

"Café Beignet," I answered.

Aimee tapped its location on the map. In this fashion, a series of purple marks appeared on the map. Some were in the heart of the French Quarter, others were simply little stops along busy streets. I stared at the map for so long that my eyes started to burn. Vance came up behind me and stared over my shoulder at the map.

"How does this help us?" my detective friend wanted to know.

I shrugged. "I thought I might be able to see a pattern."

"You don't, do you?" Vance asked.

"Nope, aside from them all being fairly close together."

"They're all close together," Jillian murmured, as she gently tapped one of the marks on Bourbon Street. "I think that might be the key you're looking for?"

"Say what?" I asked, confused.

"What was that?" Vance said, at the same time.

Jillian traced her finger along Bourbon Street before dropping it down to do the same to Royal.

"If you notice, everything here is within walking distance of one another. Also of note is the fact that we've had a person following us who was also on foot."

"How is that important?" I asked.

"Don't you see? We know food is involved, and we know the affected areas of interest are close to one another."

"Sounds like you're suggesting our perp doesn't have a car," Vance mused.

Jillian nodded. "Yes, exactly. I think … I think our mystery man might be a delivery person."

"For a restaurant?" I asked, certain I would be ridiculed for suggesting such a hypothesis. When no laughter—or teasing—manifested, I sighed with relief. I think I was beginning to see where my fiancée was going with this. "Our guy is someone who is very familiar with the city."

"Especially the French Quarter," Vance agreed. "If he's a delivery driver, er, delivery what … walker? I don't know the correct term. Whatever. If our guy works for a local restaurant, is there any way to tell which one?"

"And that must be why there are so many references to food," Tori added. "Sherlock and Watson must be trying to get us to pay attention to certain things."

I cleared my throat. "My question is, what does this guy have against me? There were bigger names at the expo than me. Why single me out?"

"He definitely seems to know who you are," Jillian recalled. "Remember the podcast? He called in and said he listened to you talk about *Heart of Éire* during the panel. That means he was somewhere in the audience, doesn't it?"

"Or, he was close enough to overhear what was being said," Vance argued.

Jillian nodded. "You have a point. Anyway, if I remember correctly, he said he was interrupted, and that there'd be another attack. Wouldn't that suggest some type of animosity toward Zachary?"

I held my hands up in mock surrender. "What animosity? What am I accused of doing? I didn't organize that expo. I'm not the one who booked the guests. I can't imagine what this guy has against me."

"Yet, he seems to think you're the one who stopped him," Vance observed. "We might be able to use that to our advantage."

I turned to my friend. "How, exactly?"

"We use you to draw him out."

"Bait? Me? I seem to recall that using a live person as bait has never really worked too well for us before," I argued. "What makes you think it'll work this time?"

Vance sat back and grinned. "My instincts. They're never wrong."

"Your instincts?" I scoffed. "All right, let's review. You originally thought I was guilty of murder …"

Aimee gasped with surprise and scooted her chair a few inches away from me. Jillian laid a hand over the girl's and shook her head no, and then rolled her eyes. Thankfully, Aimee flashed her a smile.

"... you unwisely bet against whether or not a certain piece of Egyptian jewelry could be found by a human before a certain pair of dogs could. There's also ..."

"All right, that's enough," Vance grumped. "Point made. What I'm trying to tell you is that ... is that ... hold on."

"Did you forget what you're trying to say already?" I teased. "I'm so getting you some gingko for Christmas this year."

"You guys are funny," Aimee decided.

Vance pulled out his small notebook, flipped to an empty page, and hastily scribbled a note.

"Look, I'm not trying to be paranoid here," he was saying, as he casually tore the sheet from the notebook and slid it to me, "it's just that I think this could work."

I looked down at the note and had to order myself not to respond.

I THINK THERE'S A CHANCE WE'RE BEING WATCHED. DON'T REACT.

Vance thought someone was spying on us? Who? Only a few tables were occupied out here on the patio. Of the three that were filled, one had a couple, and the other two had two small families. I could only assume Vance's finely-tuned instincts needed a tune-up.

I signaled the waiter I was ready for the check

and handed him my credit card. "Lunch is on me, so use that, if you would. Aimee, I do appreciate all your help."

The girl whipped out a pen from some concealed pocket and hastily scribbled her number on Vance's note. "Keep in touch, would you? I'd love to know how this works out."

Once we were outside, I was about to suggest we head west, back toward our hotel. The farther west you went, the fewer people you encountered. I figured it'd be easier to spot someone tailing us, provided someone *was* tailing us, that is. But, before I could say anything, I felt the leashes go taut. Sherlock and Watson, it would seem, had someplace to be.

"All right, guys. You've got the lead. Let's go. Just don't try to cut anyone off, or dart between anyone's legs, just because you can, 'kay?"

As was the case whenever the dogs have been alerted to something, I was ignored.

"Oh, man, I am so sorry. Please excuse us. Look out, coming through! This is the Corgi Express, comin' up on your six. Look out! Sherlock? I swear I'm gonna ... whoops! My bad, ma'am. No, I wasn't going to threaten my dogs. That'll happen later."

Thankfully, it didn't last long. Less than five minutes later, we came to a stop. Looking down at the dogs, I could see both of them were staring at a nearby gift shop. Slowly walking up to the perimeter of the store, I could see they had every trinket, bead, and article of clothing every other store catering to tourists had. The dogs, though, only had eyes for the displays placed just outside the front door.

"Whataya got?" Vance asked, as he appeared at my side. "Anything good?"

I pointed at the display. "You tell me. That display? It has beaded necklaces and quite the variety of Mardi Gras masks."

I felt Jillian's soft hand tap my shoulder. "Zachary? Look at Watson. She's looking at a display, too, only it isn't the same one."

Sure enough, Watson was staring at a similar display, only on the opposite side of the store. What did it have?

"Cookbooks," I breathed. I looked over at Jillian and nodded. "Cookbooks and masks. It would seem as though we need to figure out why the dogs are so interested in food."

I really shouldn't have bothered. The reason why the dogs kept zeroing in on food was so freakin' obvious that I'm surprised I didn't pick up on it earlier. But, to my credit, no one did.

NINE

M onday afternoon found us back in the hotel, but this time, we were in the recently opened giant conference room on the ground floor. What were we doing? Well, MCU—wanting to get the most bang for their buck—arranged with our hotel to rent their meeting room so that they could try again with another book signing. Joining me for this outing were Vance and Tori, of course, with Jillian and the dogs sitting nearby. At the next table over was Cassie Merryman, sitting quietly at the center of her table with stacks of books on either side. Jack Dalton and Mark Spears were also there, at their own respective tables. I should also point out that three other publishers expressed interest in pooling resources with MCU, so on the opposite side of this conference room were several more sets of tables.

I have to hand it to my publisher. They certainly knew what they were doing when it came to promotional marketing. I have no idea where they were currently running their advertisements, but it certainly had the intended effect. There was a large crowd of people waiting outside the hotel's lobby when the conference room doors opened to allow in visitors.

"Look at all of them," Vance murmured. He polished off his bottle of water and leaned back in his chair. "And all they want to do is hand you money. Wow. I could get used to doing this on a regular basis."

I turned to stare at my friend. "Really? You're comfortable speaking to groups of strangers day in and day out?"

Vance shrugged. "Sure, why not? With what they're paying us in royalties, I figure it's the least we could do."

"Don't ever let MCU hear you say that," I laughed. "They'd sign us up for a coast-to-coast book tour in less time than it takes to click a pen."

"How bad would that be?" Tori asked. "MCU pays for your hotel, your food, your travel expenses, and on top of all that, pays you monthly. Do you know what? I think I'd like to try it."

Vance looked over at his wife. "What, write a book? When are you going to have time to do that? You're always complaining about how you don't have enough free time."

"I think I can do it," Tori insisted.

Interested, I leaned forward. "What kinds of books, Tori? What genre would you pick?"

"Well, I would never want to compete with you," Tori began. "Your stories are too good. I was actually thinking more along the lines of a children's book?"

"I have several author friends who specialize in writing books for children. Say the word, and I can ask them to pass along some advice."

Tori clapped excitedly. "That would be wonderful! Thank you, Zack!"

"I should warn you, though," I cautioned, as I waggled my finger at her, "the one thing I do know about children's books is that it's a tough genre to gain your footing. But, once you do, then it's pretty much smooth sailing. Also, since most children's books are illustrated, you're going to want to think about finding someone who can illustrate your stories."

"She doesn't need to worry about that," Vance chuckled.

Tori nodded. "True story."

"One of your daughters," I guessed.

"Both, actually," Tori confirmed. "Thank you, Zack. Any and all advice you can send my way would be greatly appreciated."

"Anything for a friend."

I looked back at the rows of chairs that had been set up and spotted Jillian sitting there with the corgis. Sherlock was on her lap and Watson was curled up on the adjacent seat. Realizing I didn't want my fiancée sitting by herself, a few extra chairs were added to our table. Seeing what we were doing, Jillian nodded and hurried over.

"You're the sweetest."

"Hey, you looked like you could use some human company," I said, giving her hand a squeeze. "Plus, you need to hear the news Tori just gave me."

Jillian looked at her friend. "Oh? Oh, my! You're expecting!"

Vance snotted the water he was drinking.

"No, silly," Tori giggled. "I'm going to try my hand at writing!"

"That shouldn't be too difficult for you," Jillian decided. "You have a very active imagination. What kind of books?"

"Children's stories," Tori announced.

"Oooh, that's an excellent idea! I've often thought about cleaning up and publishing some of the stories I've written, too."

It was my turn to choke on my drink, only I had soda, of course. Thankfully, it didn't make too much of a mess this time around.

"What? You've written some stories? How come I've never known this about you?"

"You're a professional writer, Zachary. I, obviously, am not. I didn't want to waste your time by getting your input on some silly stories I wrote years ago."

"I'd really like to read some," I insisted. "All kidding aside, I'd be honored to be able to read through something you've written."

Jillian waggled a finger at me. "Only if you

promise to tell me if it truly stinks."

Talk about taking the wind out of one's sails. Perhaps this was something I shouldn't have pursued?

"Um, well …"

"Zachary Michael, if you want any chance of reading what I've written, then you need to promise me you'll be honest with me. I'm a big girl. I can take harsh criticism."

"That goes for me, too," Tori announced. "I'll accept your help only if you are completely honest with me, too."

I sat back in my chair and studied the two women.

"Dangerous ground, pal," Vance softly murmured.

I crossed my arms over my chest. "All right, fine. If you want honesty, then that's what I'll give you guys. I just don't want to hurt anyone's feelings."

"You won't," Jillian assured me. Tori met my eyes and nodded, too. "We can't get better if we don't get honest critiques."

I made a play of whipping out my phone and bringing up the voice recorder. Hitting the *Record* button, I set the phone on the table and looked expectantly at Jillian.

"Would you care to repeat that, ma'am? For the record?"

Jillian giggled, deactivated the recorder app on my phone, and slid it back to me.

"Not a chance, buster. Oh, look, Zachary. They must have unlocked the gates. Here comes the public!"

A steady stream of people filed in through the open doors. Most of the fans had already figured out which authors they wanted autographs from. Many of them were clutching books tightly to their chests. For the record, this is the exact reason I typically don't do book signings: this was nothing more than a popularity contest. If, by chance, you hadn't built up a following of fans and readers, then you were going to look silly, sitting by yourself on the opposite side of the table. It's also why I was very glad I had Jillian and the Samuelsons with me. They could keep me company in case no one showed up.

Thankfully, in this case, as the large mass of people entered the conference room and caught sight of the name placards next to our seats, the vast majority of them headed my way. I ended up taking tons of pictures with every fan who had a phone. I signed so many books that I honestly lost count. The really cool thing was how many of them were the new Ireland book. And, after announcing to the gathering masses that the reason I wrote *Heart of Éire* was sitting with me, Vance and Tori got to experience the joys of writing their own name so many times that they—quite literally—ended up misspelling them. Been there, done that.

"This is insane," Vance whispered, nearly an hour later. "My hand is hurting so bad that I'm afraid I'll end up chopping it off to give to the next person if I'm asked to sign something again. I have no idea how you can do this for so long."

I looked at Tori. "Better get used to this. Book signings will typically be either so damn popular that the time will fly, or you'll be bored out of your skull while waiting for someone to stop at your table."

"I can see why you avoid these things," Tori said, as she looked around the room. "At least the other MCU authors seem to be doing pretty good, too."

"We've got one heck of an advertising team," I said, as I signed yet another paperback copy of *Heart of Éire*. I slid the book down the table, over to Vance and Tori, so they could add their signatures next to my own. "I've been asked over and over why I don't self-publish my books. The simple fact is, I could, only I'd be responsible for handling *everything*. And let's face it, I suck at advertising. I'd much rather have someone else do it."

"Do you think I should self-publish?" Tori asked, after the latest fan wandered off with his thrice-signed book.

"If you can't find a publisher, then you most certainly could," I told my friend's wife. "And, if you still encounter problems, then all you have to do is ask. I'd be more than happy to help get your book published."

Tori laid a hand over mine. "Thanks, Zack. You're the best!"

I grinned at Vance. "Did you hear that? Huh? Your wife just said I was the best!"

"Don't let it go to your head," Vance playfully grumped, giving his wife a huge grin.

"Too late," Jillian giggled. "It already has, I'm sure."

"I can feel the love in this room," I snickered.

A group of four teenage girls approached our table. Looking up, I noticed all four couldn't have been more than sixteen. Two were blonde, one was a redhead, and the fourth was a brunette.

"Hello, ladies!" I said, as I gave the girls a smile. "What can I do for you?"

Wordlessly, they held out their copies of *Heart of Éire*.

"Would you like me to sign them? I'd be more than happy to. Plus, my friends here, Vance and Tori, would also love to sign them, seeing how they're the reason I wrote it in the first place."

"Really?" the redheaded teenager asked. "Was it their idea to set the story during Ireland's Great Potato Famine?"

"Well, no," I admitted, "but it was their idea to base it in Ireland."

All the girls giggled and shot discreet looks among themselves.

"No, we didn't," I heard Vance whisper. "I just said … oomph!"

"Just play along," I heard Tori whisper back.

"And our heroine?" I continued. "Tori? Well, meet the real-life Tori. She's the basis and inspir-

192

ation for the fictitious Tori."

The girls presented their books to us and allowed the three of us to sign them. One of the blondes, wearing a dark blue shirt and white shorts, hesitated as her three companions stepped away from our table and began heading for the next nearest table, which was Cassie's. As the three kids struck up a conversation with my fellow MCU author, I became aware of someone standing in front of me. Looking up, I offered the girl what I hoped was a genuine smile.

"Hello, there. I'll bite. You've got something else you'd like to ask me about. Well, hit me with your best shot. What can I help you with?"

"I, er, uh, am hoping to ... er, become a writer. Someday. Is there, well, I mean, could you give me any advice? For example, where do you draw your inspiration from?"

Glancing around the room, I could see there were more people waiting for signatures from the authors, but at the moment, the only person I had in front of my table was this girl. Nodding at the teenager, I sat back in my chair and pretended to think.

It was also at this time that I happened to glance down at Sherlock and Watson, fully expecting they'd be fast asleep. They weren't. Both were wide awake, and both were staring at the girl. Well, more specifically, I think they were staring at the other three girls, who had now moved on to an author who wasn't part of MCU.

"What's your name?" I asked the girl.

"Jeanette. Jeanette Dissard."

"Pleased to meet you, Jeanette Dissard. So, you're looking to become a writer?"

The girl nodded eagerly. "It's what I've always wanted to do. I've been writing stories since I was seven."

"Woof."

I glanced down at Sherlock and gave him a pat on the head. "You're a good boy, Sherlock. Hang in there, 'kay? Jeanette? Good for you. Well, the biggest piece of advice I can give you is to keep writing, every single day. It keeps those creative juices flowing."

"How do I get an agent?" Jeanette asked. I could detect a hint of frustration in her voice. "There's no clear explanation how you are supposed to find one."

"That's because most agents will require you to write them first and pitch your idea for a book. You'll never want to send in a manuscript unless they specifically ask for it up front. What you'll need to start working on is what's called a query letter."

The girl's face lit up.

"I'm so glad you brought that up! How do you write one? How are you supposed to summarize your book in less than a paragraph?"

"Been researching this, too, haven't you?" I guessed.

Jeanette nodded.

"You've been doing your homework, that's for sure," I told the girl. "Writing a query letter is very difficult. You have to introduce yourself, announce what type of book you're pitching, and then explain it in such a way that arouses their interest. You have to make them *want* to read your book."

"It's not that easy," Jeanette pouted.

I leaned forward. "Tell me about it. What I would do, if I were you, would be to look up examples of query letters online and write one based on the structure and format you find. Remember, most agents receive probably hundreds of letters each week. You'll have to make yours stand out. And finally, don't get discouraged if you're turned down. Most writers will tell you that it takes upwards of three to four months before you'll typically hear back from an agent, and ninety-nine percent of the time, you'll be turned down. As an author, you're going to have to grow some thick skin."

The girl held out a hand. "Thank you so much for your help, Mr. Anderson. I won't ever forget it!"

"I wish you the best, Jeanette. Tell you what, when you've finished your book, and if you'd like a second opinion on it, feel free to reach out to me. I'd be more than happy to take a look."

Jeanette squealed with excitement. The other three girls in her group appeared by her side.

"Woof!"

I leaned back to check out the dogs curled up at my feet. "What's the matter with you? Do you have to go outside? Can you give me five minutes?"

"He talks to his dogs all the time," I heard Vance conspiratorially tell the group of girls.

"Continuing on," I said, as I made a face at Vance, "if you choose to accept my help, then be prepared to accept the help I give as just that: help. I'm not going to go out of my way to make your life miserable. I will literally tell you what I think and what parts of your book could use more work. Be sure you can take critique for what it is and leave your personal feelings at home. Can you do that?"

The teenager beamed a smile at me. "Oh, absolutely! This is so exciting! Thank you so much!"

"You're welcome. Where are you girls off to next?"

Two in the group, the redhead and the other blonde, shrugged, as though they didn't have a care in the world. Jeanette looked back at her friends and pointed north.

"Want to get a bite to eat?"

The brunette, however, was frowning. "If we want to catch the Mighty Con before it closes down, we have to go. *Now*."

"Tina, no one wants to go see the Mighty Con," the brunette complained. "If you want to go so badly, then maybe you should just go see it yourself."

"Fine! Maybe I will!"

Tina turned on her heel and stormed off. Surprised, I looked at the three friends and hooked a thumb at Tina's retreating form.

"WOOF!"

"We're almost at a stopping point, pal," I told the corgi. "Bear with me. Jeanette? If you don't mind me asking, just what is the Mighty Con?"

"It's a comic-con," the teenager explained. "This year, they're focusing on comic books, which Tina hates."

"Then, why ask if the rest of you were going to see it?" Jillian wanted to know.

The three teens shrugged, in unison.

"Tina's always been something of a nerd," Jeanette explained. "Besides, she was a little miffed this year."

"It's not our fault the Big Easy Con was canceled this year," the second blonde girl said. "Not enough tickets were sold."

"What do they do if that happens?" I asked.

"They either cancel the show or else push it off until enough tickets *have* been sold," Jeanette answered.

Vance held up his hands in a time-out gesture. "Wait just a minute. You're telling me girls actually *want* to go to these Star Trek conventions?"

"Star Trek is so lame!" the second blonde girl cried. "Star Wars is so much better!"

"And I like you so much better now," I said, which caused the girl to blush. "Star Wars is soooo much better than Star Trek. You have excellent taste."

"I just find it hard to believe girls would be interested in that type of stuff," Vance continued, shaking his head.

Tori and Jillian regarded Vance with neutral expressions on their faces. Thankfully, Vance sensed the imminent danger he was in, and started backtracking.

"Well, okay, girls can like it too, I guess, only I haven't known many that do."

Jillian held up her hand. "I've been to five, detective. I've loved every one of them. What about you, Zachary?"

I held up four fingers. "You're one higher than me. I will admit it's been ages since I've been to one. We ought to go sometime, my dear."

"How many of those comic-cons could there be?" Vance asked, bewildered. "I'd like to believe they are only held once a year?"

I shook my head, raised my index finger, and indicated he needed to go higher.

"Two? What, three? There's no way, pal."

"There's more than you think," I told my detective friend. The three girls were nodding. "Most cities have two or three each year, and some of the bigger cities have even more than that. It's just a fun way to get together with other fans and talk about your favorite movies, television shows, and so on."

"Don't forget about dressing up as your favorite characters," Jeanette said.

I shook my head. "I won't say I'm a huge fan of dressing up, but I do enjoy watching everyone else have fun with it."

"Where's the Mighty Con being held?" Jillian asked. "Is it nearby?"

"It used to be," Jeanette confirmed, "only it's not as popular as it used to be. I don't see how they could stay in business being so far away."

"The last time a comic-con was held at the convention center, they tried *giving* tickets away," the redheaded girl said, frowning. "There were online petitions, asking them to bring the comic-cons back, only it never happened."

Jeanette sighed. "Comic-cons are so *out* right now. They need to either step up their game and get better guests or … or … I don't know. Drop the price of admission?"

Intrigued by this line of thought, I cleared my throat and waited for the girls to look my way.

"Are you suggesting that the local comic-cons were struggling? They weren't pulling in that many fans?"

All three girls nodded.

"Where're you going with this, pal?" Vance inquired.

I held up a finger as a notion occurred. "Bear with me, buddy. Jeanette? Where were the comic-cons originally held?"

Jeanette turned to point southwest. "That way. There's a big convention center that way."

I nodded. "As it happens, I'm familiar with it. Um, it wouldn't be the one that was attacked a couple of days ago, would it?"

The girls sadly nodded.

"People were poisoned there," the second blonde teen told me. "It was so sad."

"Not very mature," the redheaded girl added.

Jeanette visibly brightened, as if she was a news reporter who had just shifted from one story to the next. "At least it didn't happen when the Big Easy Con was there. That would have been horrible."

"Could someone feel bad enough about losing their favorite comic-con to a bunch of authors and readers?" I quietly asked, making sure I was loud enough for Jillian, Vance, and Tori to overhear.

"As in, enough to enact some type of retaliation for losing their venue to a book convention?" Vance asked, nodding. "I think we might have a new lead to pursue."

"Was this the big convention center right off the Mississippi?" Tori asked.

All three teens nodded.

Tori looked at Vance and offered him a sheepish smile. "Hey, I just wanted to be sure."

"Awwwwooooooo!"

Surprised, everyone at our table looked down at Sherlock and Watson. They were on their feet and eyeing the teens, as though they didn't trust them.

"What cute dogs!" Jeanette exclaimed. "What are their names?"

"Sherlock and Watson," I automatically answered. I looked over at Vance. "A comic-con was trumped by an author convention. *Our* author convention. What does that sound like to you?"

Vance's face hardened. "Motive."

"And this other location?" the second blonde continued, in mid-rant, as she crossed her thin arms across her chest. "It's tiny compared to the regular place. There's hardly any vendors, the selection of merchandise sucks, and it can only be open certain hours."

"Don't forget where it's being held now," the redhead reminded her friend.

Jeanette snapped her fingers. "That's right! It's now over twenty miles away! What kind of idiot puts a convention so far away from the city? Someone who doesn't like comic-cons, that's who. Guys? Are you ready? It was nice chatting with you, Mr. Anderson. Loved the book! Keep up the good work!"

Once the teenagers were gone, I looked at my friends and was about ready to ask if we should look into the possibility that a disgruntled fan was responsible for the attack when a certain someone finally lost his patience with me.

"Awwwooooowooooowoooo!" Sherlock angrily howled.

"What's gotten him so riled up?" Vance wanted to know, as he stepped away from the table and knelt down beside the feisty corgi. "What is it, boy? Is there something we need to see?"

The corgis were staring at the direction the girls had departed, but then I caught Sherlock looking off, toward a different door, which happened to be in the direction the fourth member of the group had gone. I figured Sherlock's logic went something like, girl number one went outside, and then so did the rest of the group. Clearly, being outside was the place to be. It had probably been a few hours since either of the dogs had been able to do their business, so I figured a potty break was due.

"All right, I'm sorry. I know you've been wanting to go outside. There, see? I'm up. Let's go outside and see if we can find a tree. I ... whoa! Hold up! What's your problem? Take it easy! We're headed outside, okay?"

Once we were outside, we saw that Tina, the grumpy brunette from before, must have been waiting outside for her friends, because we saw that the four girls were together once more. However, this time, the group of friends were arguing among themselves. Ignoring the heated debate they were having, I veered off for the closest tree, only I was surprised to feel both dogs pulling on their leashes, and I mean they were pulling on those leashes as though they thought they were oxen plowing a field. Where were they headed? Toward the girls, of course.

"Would you knock it off?" I demanded. "What could you possibly want with ..."

I trailed off as I realized a few things at the same time. Oh, don't get me wrong, I'm sure you've already realized what I missed. But, in my case, I suddenly remembered all the times Sherlock woofed inside the hotel's conference room. And, as those rusty wheels ground into motion, I remembered it started just after Tina had left to go outside. Was

Sherlock trying to tell me something? Why had he wanted me to pay attention to the one girl who left the group early?

I looked over at Tina and studied her.

"What is it?" Jillian asked, as she finally caught up with us. "You three practically ran out of there as though you were being chased by the Boogeyman himself."

I pointed over at the teens, who were still busy arguing.

"Look at them. The three of them are clearly mad at Tina, but I have no idea why. And, for that matter, it looks like Tina doesn't care in the slightest."

"You came out here to watch those girls? Whatever for?"

I pointed at the dogs. "Sherlock started woofing the moment Tina left the group. I didn't pay any attention to it at the time, but I'm thinking I should have.

Jillian's mouth formed an O of surprise. "What do you think it means?"

"I think it means Sherlock recognized her," Vance suggested, as he and Tori appeared next to my fiancée. "But from where, I don't know."

Just then, Tina looked over at us and saw us studying her and throwing in an occasional arm gesture. Seeing that we were all talking among ourselves, the teen girl said something to her friends and immediately darted away. The corgis, I should point out, wanted to pursue.

"They want us to go after her," Vance said, as he studied the dogs. "Who's that girl? What do we know about her?"

"Let's go find out," I said, as I hurried over to the three friends who looked as though they would now be perfectly happy to be a trio rather than a quartet. "Jeanette? Please pardon the interruption. Your friend, Tina? Can I ask how well you know her?"

"We've gone to school together since the second grade," Jeanette said. "Why would she say she had to get away from you? You've never met her before, have you, Mr. Anderson?"

"Not that I'm aware of," I said.

"I wonder what's wrong," the second blonde teenager said.

I pointed at Sherlock and Watson. "Well, my dogs have a way of indicating when something is amiss, and based on their reaction to your friend, they think something is wrong. Look at them. They want us to go after your friend, so I need to know what else you can tell us about her."

Jeanette shrugged. "I can tell you just about anything you'd want to know. She's a Scorpio. She's also a serious Star Wars fan, and loves that baby Yoda character from the new series on Disney's streaming service."

"The Mandalorian," I said, nodding. "Well, she's got great taste."

Jillian swatted my arm and held a finger to her lips.

"Tina has lived in New Orleans all her life. She's said to me on more than one occasion that her great-grandmother used to live just down the street from her."

The redhead snapped her fingers. "Don't forget about Gus."

Jeanette nodded. "That's right. I was just coming to that."

"Gus?" I repeated, puzzled. "Is that the name of her boyfriend?"

The three girls laughed out loud.

"No, silly," Jeanette explained. "Gus. It's actually an acronym for GS. It's her family's restaurant on St. Peter Street."

Recognizing the name of the street, I fought to keep the excitement from my voice. "Er, um, *what* restaurant? What's it called?"

"Gumbo Stop," Jeanette answered. "Tina handles all their deliveries for them."

TEN

"S he *must* be him," I said, as I followed the dogs along Royal Street, on our way back to the place where I had sampled gumbo for the first time. "And what was I thinking? Of course it's gumbo! No wonder the dogs kept stopping to look at menus. What do you want to bet that if we were to look at those pictures I took, the ones with menus on them, we would find a listing for gumbo?"

"Your mystery man?" Tori asked, as she and Vance hurried to keep up. "You think your red-haired mystery man is really a girl?"

"That explains why I always thought the man we were looking for was either slight, or short," Jillian said. She had control of Watson's leash and was expertly guiding the female corgi around people, tourist displays, and so on. "No red hair, and no tattoos. I was right. It was clearly part of the mask she was wearing."

"How sure are you it was her?" Vance wanted to know.

"Pretty sure," I said. We had been following Royal Street and had just hit the intersection with Toulouse Street. We had one more block to go before we were back at St. Peter. But, I had to rein in my steeds, or else I'd be taken out by the oncoming traffic. "She's a nerd, pal."

"What does that have to do with anything?" Vance wanted to know.

"In this case, it doesn't mean anything derogatory," I explained. "Think about it. She told us she enjoys sci-fi movies, like Star Wars. She enjoys going to comic-cons with her friends. And, speaking of comic-cons, she indicated she was not happy about having to traipse across town to get to wherever it was now being held."

"I still don't see how being a nerd is relevant," Vance said.

"Costumes," I said, as though that very word should be a sufficient explanation. "People who go to comic-cons typically like to dress up as their favorite characters."

"So?" Vance prompted.

"So, it means they're very familiar around masks, makeup, and wigs."

Tori's eyes widened. "Oh. I hadn't even thought of that. Nice job, Zack!"

I shot Vance a triumphant look. But, before he could react, the light turned green and we were allowed to cross the street. Just like that, thanks to the dogs, we were power-walking the last block before we all turned right. And ... there it was. Gumbo Stop, looking—and smelling—just like I remembered it. The four of us, standing behind the two corgis, looked at the front of the shop and then eyed each other.

"Well?" I asked. "Who gets to do the honors?"

"What honors?" Jillian asked.

I pointed at the little restaurant. "Who gets to be the one who goes in there and accuses one of their employees of sickening dozens of people ..."

"... and killing one," Tori quietly added.

"... and killing one," Jillian amended. "I can't imagine it'll go over well."

"What if she's in there?" I asked.

Vance's face turned grim. "Fine, I'll do it. But, I need to let the local boys know what we're doing first."

I watched my detective friend pull out his cell and fire off several rapid texts. While he was doing that, I kept a close eye on the dogs. After all, in case Tina was in there, and we *were* being watched, I figured the dogs would be able to track her much better than any of us could. For the time being, they were content to stay by my side and watch Gumbo Stop's front entrance.

"Want me to go with you?" I asked.

Vance turned to regard me for a few moments. "Yeah, you know what? Why not? Jillian, Tori? Take the dogs, please. Zack? You're with me."

Just before we reached the door, Vance's cell

rang. It was Detective Martins. Vance showed me the display before stepping to the side, indicating he wanted to check in with the police before venturing inside.

"Detective Martins? Detective Samuelson here. I … what's that? How'd we know to tail this Tina person? Believe it or not, the dogs have been … yes, that's right. The dogs have been dropping clues in front of us for the past few days and we finally picked up on them. Yeah, I know it sounds silly, but unless you were there, there's no way to explain that without sounding crazy."

While Vance was on the phone with the local police, I pulled my own phone up and checked the pictures I had taken for the corgis. The ones with food-related items, that is. Sure enough, gumbo was the answer. On each of the menus I had snapped a picture of, gumbo was clearly one of the offerings. Oddly enough, that included Café Beignet. Their menu just had a single line under Side Dishes: a cup of gumbo.

My eyes dropped down to the dogs. Sherlock was staring at me. In fact, I think the little booger was smirking. Watson had a look of expectation on her face, as though she was saying, *well, now you know. What are you gonna do about it?*

Dogs.

"You're kidding," I heard Vance say. Turning, I saw him slowly pacing in front of Jillian and Tori, oblivious to the passing tourists he almost collided with. "No, I didn't know that. That coincides beautifully with what we found out. Yes, sir, that's right. It pertains to our prime suspect. This girl, Tina. She works at her family's restaurant, handling deliveries. Since I can't imagine she delivers orders on foot, then I'm thinking she must have a bicycle, or a ..."

The corgis suddenly leapt to their feet and lunged forward, which caught both Jillian and Tori off guard. Both ladies were physically pulled forward, but only by a few feet. Jillian recovered quicker, and brought Sherlock to an immediate stop. Tori was a few seconds behind her.

"Now, what was that for?" Jillian asked, as she dropped into a squat next to the tri-colored corgi. "Did you see something? Smell something?"

What I hadn't realized, and didn't notice, was the departure of a pink 2011 Vespa S scooter. It squeezed through a narrow gap between Gumbo Stop and the specialty clothing store next door and headed south on St. Peter. Thanks to Sherlock and Watson's lunge in the opposite direction, we all had our backs to Gumbo Stop, which meant—of course—the driver hadn't noticed our presence. I couldn't be certain, since she was wearing a pink helmet, but I'm pretty sure it was our girl. Thankfully, Vance finished his phone call and turned around in the nick of time.

"That's her! Check out the pink scooter!"

"She obviously made it back," Jillian observed, as she shaded her eyes with her hand. "Do you see the wire basket between the handlebars? She's making a delivery."

"And she didn't see us?" I asked, amazed.

Vance studied the dogs for a few moments before offering them each several doggie biscuits. "They are something. They distracted us, Zack."

"We all turned around, so Tina didn't see us," Jillian said. "Well, she's gone. Now what? Do we try and follow?"

I pointed at the store. "If she's making a delivery, then that means she's back on the clock. It means she'll be coming back after a bit. I say we head inside. Wait. You were talking to Martins. What did he have to say?"

Vance snapped his fingers. "Oh, that's right. Hey, get this. Detective Martins and his shadow uncovered evidence that suggested whoever was responsible for the attack did so without the use of a car."

"Is that what you suggested yesterday?" I asked.

Vance nodded. "That's right. Anyway, you said Tina works here, right? Well, let's find out if the driver of that scooter was her." He turned, walked over to Gumbo Stop's front door, and held it open. "After you, pal."

Once inside, the two of us slowly looked around. Three or four tiny round wooden tables were here and there. There were two stations where customers could dump their trash, stow their trays, or else pick up some plastic flatware. But, it was clear the majority of orders were eaten outside. And, for the record, I thought it smelled fan-freakin'-tastic.

"Afternoon," a friendly voice said. Vance and I both looked at the older gentleman standing behind the counter, wearing a stained white apron and a hair net over his balding gray hair. "What can I get for you two gents today? I'm out of sausage, but the batch of seafood gumbo I made this morning is now ready. What do you say I get you guys a bowl each?"

Vance held up his hand, with his badge prominently displayed. The older man's eyes widened with alarm.

"Is everything okay? What's the matter? Why are you here?"

"Detective Vance Samuelson," Vance said, by way of answer. "This is Zack Anderson, who is a consultant of mine."

"What's going on?" the man behind the counter demanded. "Is Tina all right? Has something happened to her?"

"You're her father," I guessed.

The man hesitantly held out a hand. "Ernie Vallot."

Vance's notebook appeared in his hand. "And you're the owner here?"

Ernie began to nervously twist his white apron in his hands.

"That's right, sir. Third generation business owner. I took over from my father, who took over from his."

"Do you and your wife run this establishment

212

together?" I asked, being careful to keep my tone of voice as friendly as possible.

"My wife has passed away," Ernie sadly told me. "The only family I have left is my daughter, Tina."

Oh, swell. What we had to tell him wasn't going to go over too well. I looked over at Vance and cringed. Vance returned my look and let out a sigh.

"Your daughter, Tina," Vance began. "Does she ..."

"What's happened?" Ernie interrupted. "Please tell me she's all right."

"For now," Vance told the shop owner. "I'll be honest with you. She's managed to land herself in some trouble."

"What happened now?" Ernie demanded, growing angry. "I told her if I caught her shoplifting again, then I was going to raise hell. So, has she?"

Vance shook his head. "Shoplifted? No. At least, not that I'm aware of. However, I have to tell you she's become involved in a plot to poison a bunch of people at a recent convention."

We both watched as the blood drained from Ernie's face. "The book exposition? Oh, no! I raised my Tina better than that."

"Seems she was a wee bit disgruntled," I offered.

"At whom?" Ernie wanted to know.

I spread my hands in a helpless manner. "I can only assume she was angry with the people who booked it. Looks like the book expo was more popular than her beloved comic-cons."

"What did she do?" Ernie whispered.

"Does she have access to any kind of poisons?" Vance wanted to know.

"Poisons? She's a kid, for crying out loud. No, she wouldn't have access to any types of poison. What a horrible thing to say!"

"This restaurant," Vance began, as he made a sweeping gesture with a hand, "does it use any dangerous ingredients? Is there anything that could kill you if it isn't prepared right?"

Ernie turned to give an exaggerated look at all cooking surfaces, tools, and implements. "We use only the freshest of ingredients. There is nothing here that is toxic, nor would I ever consider it."

"How has Tina been lately?" Vance wanted to know.

Ernie sighed and leaned back against the counter. "I won't lie to you. It was hard losing her mother. Tina took it very badly. She seemed to withdraw into herself and rarely come out. But, in the last month, it looked like things were going back to normal. She started smiling again and she was hanging out with her friends."

I stared at the man who looked to be about my age. His face was etched with worry lines, he had crow's feet at the corner of his eyes, and his hair was in the process of turning completely gray. I glanced around the small restaurant and noticed a few things. Everything was clean. Everything was organized. This was someone who, from the looks of things, spent every waking moment in this place.

"How long ago did you lose her?" I softly asked.

Ernie looked at me and I could see his eyes fill. Wow. That type of pain in his eyes meant her passing had to have been fairly recent.

"Two months," Ernie whispered.

"It'll get better, pal," I told him. "You'll never completely get over her, but time will help you deal with the pain. Let your daughter help you, if she can."

Ernie nodded. "Tina is my rock. I don't know what I'd do without her. You ... you lost your wife?"

I nodded. "A few years ago. And do you know what?" I tapped my chest. "I still feel her, right here. I still miss her, every day. But, as the days went by, I started to find it easier to get out of bed, to breathe, to *live*. Stay strong, pal. It'll get better."

A tear escaped from Ernie's right eye and rolled down his face. He used the back of a hand to wipe it away.

"Thanks."

I watched Ernie take a deep breath. Color was starting to return to his cheeks. He looked at me, and then over at Vance.

"What has she done? How can I help?"

"We need some information about your daughter," Vance began, as he pulled out his notebook. "First off, are we on the right track? Does your daughter enjoy going to comic-cons?"

Ernie nodded. "Her favorite type of books are

science fiction. She loves to imagine what life might be like on other planets. She and her mother used to go to those things all the time."

"Dressed up?" I guessed.

Ernie nodded. "That's right. How'd you know?"

"It's a lucky guess."

"I know how much Tina loves going, but I just haven't had time to take her," Ernie lamented. "What a horrible father you must think I am."

Vance looked imploringly at me and then in Ernie's direction. It would seem my detective friend wanted me in the role of sympathetic friend.

"Not at all," I told Ernie. I pointed at the restaurant. "You seem to be doing pretty good here."

"It's a struggle," Ernie admitted. "Supply prices keep going up. If I raise prices accordingly, then sales drop. You. You said you're a detective?"

Vance nodded. He displayed his badge a second time.

"If you're here, asking about Tina, that could only mean you're correct, and she's guilty. I just don't understand why. Why would she do that?"

"If the book expo looks bad," I began, "then perhaps the convention center could go back to hosting comic-cons instead? That's the only thing we could think of."

"That makes no sense whatsoever," Ernie insisted.

I nodded. "I'd agree with you. However, what if you're a fourteen-year-old girl? That's the type of

<verbumm™>216</verbumm™>

mentality she has at the moment."

"She's sixteen," Ernie corrected. He wiped his hands on his apron and pulled out his phone. "She should have been back by now. I'm going to call her. She never ignores a call from me."

Thirty seconds later, Ernie angrily shoved his cell back into his pocket.

"She's ignoring me! Why? She's *never* done that before!" Ernie dug the phone out again. Again, the call was ignored. Exasperated, Ernie waited a full thirty seconds before calling a third time.

"Tina? What are you doing ignoring me? You know the rules! Since when have you ... no you don't. There will be no interrupting me, young lady. Where are you? What's going on? Why haven't you returned yet? The police? Yeah, they're here. They're asking about you. What have you done?"

Vance and I shared a brief look.

"Christina Marie, stop this nonsense now. Come back here. You need to let these people know that you ... no! Absolutely not! You will not ... she ... she h-hung up on me!"

"Hey, she's scared," I offered. "You told her the police were here, and she probably freaked. That's why we need to find her. Did she go out on a delivery? By any chance, was it on a Vespa?"

"Her mother and I bought that for her last summer," Ernie confided. "A pink Vespa. Tina added the basket and convinced me to allow her to make deliveries for the store. Truth be told, if she hadn't, then I suspect Gumbo Stop would have folded last winter."

"People love it when food is brought to them," I said. "Tina sounds like a smart kid. Trust me when I say we want to help her. So, what else can you tell us about her?"

"What else do you want to know?" Ernie asked. His phone suddenly beeped, which had him pulling it out to inspect the screen. "Pardon me for a moment. I have an order to fill. Another of Tina's ideas. People can order food directly from their phones now."

I looked out the front window, at the building on the other side of the street. Like this one, it was two stories high. I squinted at the second story and caught sight of furniture on patios, people were walking in and out of sight, holding drinks, food, and so on. The second story? It looked residential.

I nudged Vance and inclined my head outside.

"Ernie? By any chance, do you and Tina live upstairs? Like, directly above this place?"

Ernie nodded. "We do. Why?"

"It's imperative we locate Tina as soon as possible," Vance said. I watched as his eyes hardened and his face became impassive. "Would you mind if we looked around her room?"

"Do you have a warrant?" Ernie asked, growing nervous and withdrawn again.

"No one has a warrant," I interjected, before either Vance or poor Ernie could say anything. "We're trying to help. Tina is acting distraught enough to make us think she might try to hurt someone else. She needs help. Let us give it to her, okay?"

Ernie reached into another pocket and produced a set of keys.

"Fine. Go through that door, there. At the end of the hallway, you'll find stairs going up. The silver key unlocks the door. Do what you need to do."

I sent off a quick text to the girls, telling them to meet us at the door leading into the hallway mentioned by Ernie.

"I must be slipping," Vance quietly told me, as we stepped into the narrow corridor and headed toward the street. "I didn't even know this was here."

I followed Vance to a simple glass door leading outside to the street. Since it was used by tenants to access the upper residential floors, the door was locked from the outside. Pushing it open, Jillian and Tori, still leading the dogs, followed us in.

"Do we have permission to do this?" Jillian quietly asked, as she watched Vance fumble with the keys at the top of the stairs. "I wouldn't want to go in there uninvited."

"The owner of the store is the girl's father," I explained. "He gave us permission. Tina is the only family he has at the moment, so he naturally doesn't want anything to happen to her. We're allowed to do whatever we want in there."

Vance unlocked the apartment door and stepped out of the way. The interior of the apartment was just as I expected for someone who had recently lost their significant other: cluttered chaos. Dirty dishes were stacked in the sink. Mail lay in piles on the kitchen table, unopened and unread.

Jillian and Tori both held a hand over their noses.

"What's that smell?" Jillian wanted to know.

"Smells like garbage," I decided. "I'll bet he hasn't taken the trash out for a while."

"Why would Tina want to live like this?" Tori asked. "You'd think she'd pitch in and help."

"Because of the father," I said. "He needs to pull himself together. If he doesn't take care of himself, then Tina is obviously thinking she doesn't have to, either. Or … or she feels she shouldn't have to take care of her dad. And do you know what? She's right. It should be the other way around. They're stuck in a dangerous cycle. This family needs help."

Vance ducked through a hallway. "In here. I found the girl's room. Zack, I think you're right, buddy."

We all stepped into Tina's room and came to an immediate stop. This one room was the exact polar opposite of the rest of the apartment. For starters, it was clean! The bed was made, there were no dirty clothes on the floor, and all her possessions were neatly displayed on bookcases and display racks. And, speaking of possessions, we were right. Well, the dogs were right. Tina was a fan of comic-cons, no doubt about it. Everywhere I looked, I could see Star Wars knick-knacks and memorabilia. And, based on the closest circular all-glass display, this girl was into action figures.

"Remind you of anyone?" Jillian said, as she appeared beside me.

In my house, back home, I have one of my guest rooms converted to a hobby room. Like Tina, I'm a huge fan of Star Wars. Unlike Tina, I will *not* dress up as my favorite characters. Based on the number of framed pictures on Tina's desk and on the wall, this girl loved costumes. The desk, alone, must've had at least a dozen different framed five-by-seven photographs. One had Tina decked out in all blue, with tentacles hanging off her head. Any Star Wars fan will recognize the dancing girl from Jabba's palace. You know, the one who was eaten by the Rancor?

"Wow, you should see this," Jillian said. She was standing in front of a small sliding-door closet and was staring at the clothes that were hanging up. "There's something you don't see every day. Zachary? How many can you identify?"

"What are you talking about?" I asked, as I joined Jillian at the closet. She wanted me to identify something? Then, some very recognizable outfits caught my eye. "This girl has spent some bucks on costumes, that's for sure. See the orange one? That's the X-Wing fighter pilot uniform. Then that one there? That's the outfit for a colonial warrior."

"Which movie is that from?" Vance wanted to

know.

"No movie," I said, shaking my head. "That's from the classic Battlestar Galactica TV series. And that one? Hmm. I know I've seen it before. I'm trying to picture where I've seen it."

"Imagine it on Karen Gillan," Jillian quietly suggested, "in the role of Nebula, for the Marvel movie …"

"… *Guardians of the Galaxy*," I finished.

"Jillian?" I heard Tori say. "Could you come over here for a second?"

Vance and I turned to see Tori, holding both of the dogs' leashes, standing at the window, facing St. Peter Street. She was studying a potted plant, sitting on the floor. The plant itself was about four feet high, had green leaves and red stems. Also visible were clusters of dark red berries. For the record, both Sherlock and Watson were staring at it so intently that they were acting like they expected it to sprout legs and start walking around.

"Can you identify it?" Tori asked. "I caught these two looking at it and I wanted to see if there was any significance to its presence here."

Jillian approached the potted plant and squatted down next to it. She was silent for a few moments, then she straightened, retrieved a pencil from the desk, and then gently pulled several stems this way and that. Finally, after a few moments, Jillian straightened and looked over at us. More specifically, she caught Vance's eyes and held them.

"This is pokeweed."

"You say that as though I know what it is," Vance returned. "So ... what is it?"

"It's a common source of food for songbirds," Jillian began.

"Isn't that a weird plant to have in one's bedroom?" I asked.

"Knowing this girl, I'd say it was because this plant goes by another name," Jillian said.

"And what would that be?" Vance asked.

"Dragonberries."

"Cool name," I decided. "Still doesn't explain what it's doing here."

"Let me finish," Jillian said. "Dragonberries, or pokeweed, may be food for birds, but it's toxic to humans and dogs."

Tori automatically pulled the dogs away from the plant.

"How toxic?" Vance wanted to know. He pointed at a few of the berries. "Could something like this have been used to poison, say, a bunch of people at a convention?"

Jillian nodded. "Very easily."

Vance squatted next to the plant and fell silent.

"So, this is what she used to poison people. This just keeps getting worse for her."

"Woof."

All four of us, along with Watson, turned to look at Sherlock. My tri-colored corgi was now staring at Tina's bed and was pulling on his leash. It would seem he wanted a closer inspection. Tori held out his leash.

"What is it, boy?" I asked, as I took possession of the dog. "Is there something over here you want to see?"

Sherlock pulled me over to the twin-sized bed. Figuring he'd picked up something from under the bed, I dropped to my knees and started to lower myself into position. That was when I noticed Sherlock wasn't looking under the bed, but at the junction of the two mattresses. Was there something *between* them?

"Vance? Grab that side, would you? Very slowly now, let's pick this up. I want to see what's between them."

Nodding, Vance took the back right corner and I took the front. We lifted the right side, just enough to see what could have been there. I was halfway expecting to find a few adult magazines there, but then again, this was also a girl's room. I really didn't know what to expect. However, I should've known what we'd find.

"Well, well," Vance said, sounding smug. "Look at what we just found."

An ear-splitting bark ripped through the quiet confines of the apartment.

"As I was saying," Vance hastily amended, "look at what the dogs found."

"What is it?" Tori asked, as she peered around her husband's body to see for herself. "Oh! Isn't that ...?"

"It's the mask!" Jillian exclaimed.

We let the mattress plunk back down as we stepped away from Tina's bed. Using a tissue from a nearby box, Vance had picked up the mask and was holding it as though he was a hunter, displaying the corpse of his hard-fought prey.

"Just what do you think you are doing here?" a shrill voice suddenly demanded.

The four of us whirled around. Both Sherlock and Watson began barking. Tina, it would seem, had returned from her deliveries and figured she could avoid the police by hiding in her home. Little did she know that the police were already here.

"Who are you? I'm calling the police right now!"

Vance held up the mask and then reached inside his back pocket and showed the teenager his police badge.

"I think calling the police right now would be a fantastic idea. In fact, I should tell you I sent off several messages the moment we found your mask."

Tina squealed with alarm and bolted for the door. However, before she could make it, her father appeared in the doorway, arms crossed and looking exceedingly angry.

"Dad! I can explain!"

"They walked in, leveling accusations at you," Ernie began, his tone deceptively calm. "I didn't believe them. *Couldn't* believe them."

"Dad, I ..."

"They said you had poisoned some people at a book expo," Ernie interrupted, growing red in the face. "Would that be the same one I've heard about on the news?"

Tina's face fell and she began sobbing.

"Then," Ernie continued, oblivious to the fact that his daughter had turned on the waterworks, "these people said that someone died during the attack. Christina, that was you? You killed someone?"

"I d-did no s-such thing!" Tina sobbed.

"Point of fact," Vance hastily added, "but you did. One of the fans. An innocent. How does that make you feel?"

I raised a hand and tapped my chest. "The guy who died? He had puncture marks on his chest. He wasn't poisoned. At least, I don't think he was."

Vance shrugged. "Collateral damage, then. If she hadn't created the panic, then our victim probably wouldn't have been stabbed."

"But, I didn't kill anyone! I only put in enough berries to make people sick. I wanted to make people afraid to go to that stupid book show."

"I was part of that book show," I pointed out. "I never did anything to you, yet you seemingly targeted me. There were more well-known people there than I was, yet you fixated on me. Why?"

"I just happened to be walking by when you and the dogs arrived," Tina answered, renewing her sobbing. "I was mad at the expo, not you. It's not fair! That convention center? They were hosting comic-cons long before some dumb book expo ever thought about hosting an event. Let the expo be held miles and miles away. Let the expo suffer poor ticket sales. Let's see how many guests will show up if there's no money to pay the stars."

"This is about those damn comic book shows?" Ernie practically shouted. "You did all of this just so you can play dress-up again? You need to grow up, girl!"

Tina sobbed harder.

"It's tough losing a parent," Jillian softly told the girl. "I can't even begin to imagine what you must be going through."

Tina collapsed to the floor, crying hysterically. Jillian rushed forward to pull the girl into a hug. Before anyone could say anything, we saw both Sherlock and Watson perk up. Their erect ears swiveled back and forth, as though they alone could hear something we could not. Not two seconds later, a police siren sounded, and grew steadily louder.

"Did you use the pokeweed to poison the people at the expo?" Jillian asked.

The girl nodded, her tear-streaked face looking sadder than I would have thought possible. If ever a girl could pull off wretched or miserable, this was the one.

"I added several of my dragonberries into the lunch order for the expo."

"You sabotaged my gumbo?" her father cried. "Why would you try to ruin me, Christina? Do you have any idea what's going to happen? I'll be arrested!"

Right on cue, Detective Martins arrived, with three other officers in tow. He took one look at the girl sobbing on the floor and looked questioningly at Vance.

"This? This is our suspect?"

Vance held up the rubber mask. "Yes."

Detective Martins' face hardened. "You found the mask. Did you have a warrant to search this place?"

"No. The resident gave permission to search."

Martins turned to Ernie. "Is this true, sir?"

"It's true. They indicated my daughter was involved, and I gave them my house keys."

Since I was standing closest to Ernie, Vance tossed the keys to me.

"Here they are," I said, presenting them to Ernie. "Thank you for letting us look."

Tina's tear-streaked face turned to look accusingly at her father. "You? You really let them in here? Why, Dad? Why would you do that?"

"Why would you harm innocent people?" her father countered.

When Tina didn't respond, Detective Martins snapped on a pair of gloves and carefully took the mask from Vance. He held it up in front of the girl.

"Were you wearing this several days ago, at the book expo held at the Ernest Morial Convention Center?"

Tina slowly nodded.

"You dropped a voodoo doll for everyone to see," Detective Martins angrily continued. "Why?

All I have to do is look around your home to see that you are not affiliated with that religion. Why insinuate that voodoo was involved?"

"It was a gathering of a bunch of book lovers," Tina sullenly responded. "Why not give them something to write about?"

"Do you have any idea how badly this reflects on our city?" Detective Martins snapped.

An angry look of defiance appeared on Tina's face and I could see that she was done talking. That's when I looked down at the dogs, only to find them staring straight at the girl. A flashback to the podcast from a few days ago had me gasping with alarm.

"What is it?" Jillian whispered. "Are you all right?"

I strode over to the girl and tried to stare her down. "You said there'd be a second attack. Where will it happen? What did you do? Tell us that it was just a bluff."

"The comic-cons will return once tonight is over," Tina said, raising her head to look at me. "Enjoy your popularity while you still can."

"What did you do?" Ernie demanded. "Christina Marie, you will tell us what you've done, and you will do so *now*!"

A smirk appeared on the girl's face. One thing was clear. A second attack was going to happen, and she wasn't going to help us. We were on our own.

ELEVEN

W here do we even start?" Jillian asked, as we stepped outside, onto St. Peter Street. "That poor girl is going to create another attack. We have to stop it!"

"I would agree," Vance said, as he and Tori joined us on the sidewalk. My detective friend squatted low and draped an arm around both corgis. "You two are my secret weapons. We need to know where to go, guys. Look, here are my last two doggie biscuits. Will you help us out?"

Sherlock snatched the treat from Vance's hand, while Watson timidly took the goodie as gently as she could. Once both of the corgis had dispatched their treats, they rose to their feet.

"I don't like this," Detective Martins announced, as he joined our group. "I don't like this one bit. Who knows what that whack-a-doodle girl has gone and done? Perhaps this time she's hoping for more than one casualty?"

"She claimed she wasn't responsible for killing that poor fellow from before," Jillian reminded everyone. "Personally, I believe her. Oh, don't get me wrong, that is one severely disturbed girl, but I don't think she meant to seriously hurt anyone."

"But, what's to stop her this time around?" I asked.

Jillian shrugged helplessly.

"What else could she possibly do to make the book expo look unfavorable in the public's eye?" Greg Plinth chimed in. The consultant was given a dour look from Martins, and immediately clammed up.

"The expo is over," I said, frowning. "My publisher held an impromptu signing at my hotel, but it sure couldn't have been considered an expo."

"Something's up," Martins decided. He pulled out his cell. "Let me make a few phone calls. Maybe there's something else going on."

A few minutes later, we had our answer. The convention center, realizing that it had received some bad press in the last couple of days, was donating a final night for the book expo. They were even waiving all fees and profits they'd make renting tables, provided they could jam as many people as they could into the expo. It would seem they were desperate to prove that their facility was perfectly safe. I could only hope they were right.

"It has to be it," Vance decided. "The book expo is now going to go for one more night? That must be what the girl will be targeting. We just have to figure out how, and in what way. That's the only way we're going to be able to stop her."

Detective Martins nodded solemnly before looking down at the dogs. Giving off the appearance he was having the mother of all internal debates, Martins finally swallowed his pride and asked what had to be the inevitable question.

"Er, do you think you could see about having your dogs locate whatever device is going to be used to attack the expo? The Ernest Morial Convention Center has over a million square feet of contiguous space. Finding some type of device in there will be like finding a needle in a haystack."

"A needle in a haystack would be easier to find," I muttered. I looked down at Sherlock and Watson. "Do you really think my dogs can find whatever it is you're looking for?"

"The captain has spread some seriously amazing rumors about those two dogs," Martins admitted. "He told us all about Sherlock and Watson, and their … *exploits* in Pomme Valley. As such, he's willing to renegotiate in order to enlist your help."

"Renegotiate?" Vance said, shaking his head. "You don't need to do that. I'm sure Zack and I will be able to … Zack? What are you doing?"

I had my phone in my hand and was busy typing out a string of commands. "Give me a second."

"Are you really going to negotiate some type of fee to ensure our help?" Jillian asked, frowning. "That's not like you, Zachary."

I smiled and presented my phone to my fiancée.

Jillian's lovely features broke out into a smile. "I stand corrected. Now *this* is just like you."

Vance came up behind me and looked over my shoulder. He saw what was on my phone and snorted with laughter.

"What?" Martins demanded. "What are you looking at?"

"We'll help in every way we can," I told the New Orleans detective.

"Thank you, Mr. Anderson."

"Oh, don't thank me yet. There's a price, of course."

"And that would be?" Martins suspiciously asked.

"It's easy. You and your consultant, Mr. Plinth, will be partaking in a food challenge of my choosing. And, looking up what's popular in New Orleans, there are quite a few to choose from."

Detective Martins actually laughed out loud. "Bring it on. I've actually competed in a few challenges in my day, so there's nothing you can ..."

"I've chosen the Tchoupitoulas Sundae Challenge."

Just as I expected, Martins grinned. "That's fine. I know all about that ice cream challenge. I'm sure the two of us can polish off that sundae."

"Oh, no you don't," I said, laughing. "That's one sundae for each of you."

To give you some context, the Tchoupitoulas challenge consisted of an enormous ice cream sundae, with eight scoops of ice cream, eight different toppings, and served in a huge bowl with wafers, sprinkles, and whipped cream. Yes, I could easily have made them enter the other contest I found, which was the Bayou Beast Challenge. That one involved consuming ten spicy chicken wings, all without benefit of other food, water, liquids, or even napkins, for that matter. Get those down in five minutes, and you win the challenge. It also required participants to sign a medical waiver.

And now you know why I didn't choose that one.

"You're on," Martins said, grinning. He held out a hand. "Now, what do you say we find out what this crackpot teenager was up to and make sure we put a stop to it?"

Nodding, I pulled my cell out and called MCU. Richard answered on the first ring.

"Zack? Where have you been? I've been calling and calling!"

I checked my phone, but I didn't see any mention of missed calls.

"Didn't miss anything on my end," I told Richard. "Hey, what can you tell me about ..."

"Zachary!" Richard practically shouted into the phone. "You need to listen to me!"

"I *am* listening to you," I returned. "It's kinda hard not to when you're yelling at me. Now, what I wanted to know is, the book expo? Are there any other ..."

"Will. You. Be. Quiet!"

"What's the matter?" I hesitantly asked, growing concerned.

"That's what I'm trying to tell you," Richard huffed. All of a sudden, it sounded like he was out of breath. "MCU has been invited to participate in a last minute convention. The convention center must've felt bad after what happened, because now they're offering to waive all fees if we'd be willing to give it another go."

"Yeah, I know. One of the local cops just told us."

"You're planning on going?"

"As a matter of fact, I am. Surprising, huh? Well, there's another reason to take into consideration, since ..."

"Zack, we have a problem," Richard interrupted, the moment I took a breath.

"What's the problem, Richard?"

"What's going on?" I heard Detective Martins ask, from behind me.

"Richard? Just a moment. Detective Martins? We're about ready to head over to the convention center. How many extra pairs of eyes can you give us?"

Martins stared at me for a few moments before stepping away to make a few more calls. Once the detective had wandered off, I unmuted my cell and returned to my call.

"Richard? Yeah, sorry 'bout that. The local police have asked us to help determine how someone could pull off another ..."

"Zack? I'm sorry to interrupt, but you really need to hear this."

At the exact moment my MCU contact said that, Martins, having finished his phone call and on his way back to me, received another call. This one brought the detective to an immediate stop. It even had him slapping his free hand over his ear. He quickly turned and hurried away.

"All right, hit me with your best, Richard. What's so important?"

"Did you send a threatening message to the convention center?"

Of all things my MCU rep could have said, that wasn't anywhere on the list.

"What are you talking about? I did no such thing."

"Zack, they have a recording!"

"What?!"

Apparently, I said that with enough animosity that everyone in our group stopped what they were doing and wandered close. Even Detective Martins must have heard my little outburst, because he was back in less than ten seconds.

I angrily shook my head. "What are you talking about? I did no such thing."

"You threatened everyone at the convention center," Richard insisted. "The cops aren't going to take that too lightly."

"Richard, I did no such thing," I insisted. "And I'm standing in front of the cops right now. No one has said anything about some type of recorded threat."

"Mr. Anderson?" Detective Martins said, as he

pointed at my phone. "I'm going to need you to finish your call. Something has just come up."

"Is it about some alleged threat?" I asked, growing angry. "Trust me when I said I did no such thing."

"I'm inclined to believe you," Martins told me. He held up his cell. "They sent the recording to me. Once you hear it, you'll see why we don't believe it. Granted, I realize I'm racially profiling you, but … well, just see for yourself."

Nodding, I told Richard I'd call him back when all of this was said and done. I huddled close to the detective, as did Jillian and the rest of my entourage. Martins nodded, tapped a few icons on his screen, then stepped back. A digital file began playing, and damned if it wasn't my own voice doing the talking.

The attack will happen today. Devil's Breath will rain down on you all. All hail goddess Oya.

I was frowning even before the recording finished. "Wow, what an amateur. All hail goddess Oya? Oh, yeah. That sounds like me."

"What do you mean?" Detective Martins asked.

"Well, listen to that statement. It doesn't flow well. The grammar isn't the greatest. I mean, for crying out loud, all hail goddess Oya? Seriously?"

"It was spliced together," Vance said, coming to my aid. "Anyone can tell that."

"Spliced from what?" the detective wanted to know.

I snapped my fingers. "We already know Tina is

a nerd, which means she's undoubtedly good on a computer. Tech savvy, as I believe the saying goes. We know she's responsible for the first attack, which means she was the mystery caller on Charlie Goodman's podcast. The podcast might not be currently available to download, but Tina watched it live. That meant she more than likely recorded it on her computer."

"For those of us who aren't tech savvy," Martins said, exasperated, "translate that into English, okay?"

"The girl recorded everything Zachary said onto her computer," Jillian explained, joining the conversation. "Working with digital files is relatively easy if you have the right software. Grab this word here, put it next to that word there, and you can come up with something completely different, all using the host's voice."

"I hate computers," Martins growled.

"The only question I have is, when did you mention devil's breath?" Jillian wanted to know.

"I'm pretty sure I didn't," I argued. "But, I think I remember using devil in some fashion. Clearly, I said breath, too. By the way, what *is* devil's breath? It sounds like one of those unreal potion ingredients. You know, wing of bat, eye of newt, and so on."

Jillian shook her head. "Believe it or not, devil's breath is real, and it's probably one of the most dangerous drugs on the planet."

"How do you know so much about it?" I asked,

as I turned to Jillian. "Is this something you can grow?"

Jillian shook her head and held up her phone. "Because I looked it up just as soon as I heard the name. That's just it. I've heard of it, but didn't know what it was used for. Now that I do, trust me when I say that this is bad."

Detective Martins came up to Jillian and held out a hand. "Would you mind?"

Jillian nodded and passed her phone to him. The New Orleans detective skimmed through the facts on Jillian's phone and, I'm sorry to say, the blood drained from his face. He returned Jillian's phone and hastily pulled out his own to start making calls.

"What is this stuff?" Vance wanted to know, as he lowered his voice. "Does it cause something bad to happen?"

Jillian shrugged. "It's more like, what *won't* it cause? Let's see, there's blurred vision, dizziness, dry mouth, and even urinary retention."

Vance and I flinched at the exact same time.

"Sounds miserable," Vance decided.

"Oh, I wasn't done," Jillian sighed. "According to the data I just read, if you overdose on devil's breath, then you're looking at a dangerously high heart rate, hallucinations, confusion, and a very strong likelihood that you'll fall into a coma."

"How is it administered?" Vance asked, dropping his voice down to a whisper.

Jillian pulled out her phone and tapped the

screen.

"Just a moment. I think I saw … yes. Here we go. It says, for medicinal purposes, you'd use a trans-dermal patch. If it's not being administered by a medical professional, then it can be taken orally, or through an intravenous drip, or even as a topical drug."

"Orally," Vance groaned. "Of course it'd be orally."

"You seem to be the bearer of good news," I joked, letting out a nervous chuckle. I playfully nudged Jillian in the ribs, only she wasn't smiling. No one else was. Shrugging, I held up a finger, indicating I wanted Vance to wait. Looking over at Detective Martins, I caught his eye and motioned him over.

"What is it?" Martins inquired, the instant he joined us.

"I wanted to let you know that we're all going to head over to the convention center. We've got our work cut out for us."

Martins nodded. "I'll see you there."

Once we called for a larger ride-sharing vehicle, and were speeding along Royal Street, heading to the convention center, the ramifications of what we were up against started to sink in. I looked at Jillian, squeezed her hand, and then looked down at the dogs.

"I'm thinking maybe you should take the dogs and find someplace else to be?"

Jillian shook her head. "Absolutely not. We're in

this together."

"Don't forget what you told us this stuff will do to you," I reminded Jillian. "It's not something you want to mess around with."

Jillian shook her head. "I haven't."

"And you're not worried?" I demanded.

"I heard her say what it can do," Vance added, "and have no problems going on record to say that I'm worried."

"You are?" Tori asked, concerned. "I don't like the idea of you two risking your lives ..."

"Lower your voice," Vance hastily whispered. He nodded his head at the driver, who was now using every opportunity to stare at us in his rear-view mirror. "I'm not crazy about it, either, but someone has to deal with this problem."

"You haven't heard why I'm not worried," Jillian calmly informed us.

Everyone in the van, with the exception of Jillian herself and the driver, turned to stare at her as if she was now speaking in tongues, and that included the corgis. After a few moments, I gave a little cough.

"Let's hear it. What did you notice that no one else did?"

"This, er, item which is supposedly being used? We all know it's not something to be messed with. Then again, the same could be said for those berries. I'd like to think a teenage girl wouldn't want to do, er, something like this, but then again, since when have kids ever behaved rationally? She's threatened the lives of everyone in that hotel, so …"

We all heard a gasp come from the driver.

"It's this role-playing game we're all involved in," I joked, as I plastered a huge smile on my face. "Pay no attention to us."

The driver's concerned eyes held mine a few moments longer before returning to the road.

"I doubt very much she'll use poison again," Vance said, drawing nods of approval from the rest of us. "It's too obvious. You said she's tech savvy? That means she's smart, so we can clearly …"

"… not choose the wine in front of you," I interrupted, with a smile.

Vance stared at me. "How do I know that line?"

"Princess Bride," Tori, Jillian, and I echoed.

"Ah. I've got it now. The challenge of wits. Anyway, as I was saying, she's probably noticed for herself that it's going to be impossible for her to get her hands on this drug, but that doesn't mean she can't make people *think* she has it."

"Whether she has it, or doesn't have it," Tori said, "you have to assume she does. You don't want to be caught unaware."

Vance nodded. "Exactly. All right, here we are. Everyone out. Thanks for the lift, buddy."

The driver didn't say a word. He sped out of sight the instant the loading door slid closed. Also of note was the fact that both Sherlock and Watson started pulling on their leashes the moment their paws touched the ground. Encouraged, I gave them some slack in their leashes and headed off.

"Man, that was quick," Vance observed. "Oh, I hope they can work their magic here. This is something you don't mess with, Zack."

"Don't I know it. That's one messed-up girl. I just wish I knew how she was planning on making us look bad."

"What do you mean?" Vance asked. "Why did you say that?"

"It's something the girl said," I explained, frowning. "She claimed there'd be no more book expos after tonight. That would suggest that she's somehow found a way to make us authors, or anyone associated with writers, look bad."

"Why would an author cooperate with a raving lunatic?" Jillian wanted to know.

I shrugged. "Haven't a clue, I'm afraid."

We followed the dogs as they led us deeper into the convention center. Detective Martins was right. This place was astronomically huge. There was no way we were going to thwart whatever Tina was planning on our own. I just had to hope the corgis were up to the challenge.

We passed by the large room where MCU had held their panel a few days ago. Sherlock and Watson, with their noses to the ground, ignored the room and continued down the hall, until we emerged into the food court. Briefly wondering if our working theory was wrong, and Tina had somehow planned on poisoning the attendees once more, the corgis veered left, into yet another hallway.

"We are so getting lost in here," I muttered.

"Bite your tongue," Vance ordered. "You keep your directionally challenged senses to yourself, got it?"

"Seeing how I seem to be sharing them with you, I won't complain."

"Bite me, Zack."

Precisely ten seconds later, the dogs came to a stop. The four of us were standing before a large, spinning, wire display of books. Adding to the confusion was the simple fact that I couldn't recognize any of the titles or authors. At least, that's what I thought, until I noticed a copy of *Heart of Éire*. Why would the corgis show us this?

"So, one of my books has been mixed in with the others," I told Sherlock and Watson. "What does that have to do with anything? Can we go now?"

The dogs didn't budge.

"What's up?" Vance wanted to know.

I pointed out the book. "They want to show me my own book. I just don't know why."

Jillian appeared at my side. She was silent as she studied the scene.

"Are the other MCU authors going to be here?"

I shrugged. "I think so. Why?"

Jillian pointed at my book. "Well, maybe the dogs are suggesting that Tina is determined to make you and your publisher look bad?"

Taking a quick picture of the book display, I gave the leashes some slack. Just like that, we were off. A few minutes later, we stopped again. This time, I have to admit that I was surprised. I mean, really surprised. Standing before us was none other than Cassie Merryman, one of my fellow MCU authors. She had apparently just arrived and was setting up several displays of her books on either side of her table. Sensing movement, she turned to find the four of us, with Sherlock and Watson sitting complacently at our feet, watching her intently.

"Mr. Anderson! What a surprise! Is there something I can do for you?"

I looked down at Sherlock.

"All right, pal. Jillian seems to think MCU is involved. What do you want us to see?"

All either of the corgis did was watch my fellow author like a hawk, as though they expected her to pull doggie biscuits out of thin air.

"I said it last Friday, and I'll say it again: you've got some adorable dogs, Mr. Anderson."

"Please, call me Zack," I said. "And thanks. Sherlock? Watson? Now what?"

Neither dog did anything, as though they had run out of energy. In fact, both slid from their seated positions onto the floor, in proper Sphinx-like form. I looked back at my friends and helplessly held up my hands. What were we supposed to do now?

We heard a slight commotion coming from the other side of the fabric divider, separating Cassie from the next author over. Both corgis were on their feet in a flash and both started firing off warning woofs. Curious as to who was on the other side of the fabric wall, Vance took a few steps back and leaned around the corner.

"Hey, don't mind me. We're just trying to find out who—or what—our dogs are barking at."

"Who is it?" I asked.

"He's one of the other MCU authors," Vance reported. "The older one."

"The older one," I heard a friendly voice scoff. "Thanks a lot."

"Jack? Is that you?"

"None other. Damn, Anderson, you're two for two. How in the world did they get you here for a second time?"

I wandered around the corner, still holding Sherlock's leash. The rest of the group followed. I also feel I should mention both dogs had perked up at the sound of Jack's voice, and now were straining like crazy to make it over to him. Right about that same time, Jillian's phone rang. She handed me Watson's leash and stepped off to the side to answer the call.

"Would you two knock it off? Look, it's just Jack. He's not the bad guy."

"Not the bad guy?" Jack repeated, curious. "Dare I ask what that's supposed to mean?"

Before I could answer, Sherlock and Watson switched to their Clydesdale personas and physically yanked me the final ten feet or so to arrive, breathless, at Jack's table. That's also when I noticed there were a variety of packages next to Jack's assortment of books he had brought with him. Catching sight of the first package, I pointed at it.

"What's that? Looks like it's addressed to Mark Spears."

Jack snapped his fingers. "That's right. I was the first of us to appear, so they gave them to me to hold. It looks as though they're gifts, from fans."

Gifts from fans? I caught sight of a package addressed to Jack and glanced down at the dogs. As near as I could tell, they were staring directly at Jack's gift.

Right about this time, a swarm of uniformed officers suddenly appeared, led by none other than Detective Martins. This time, his sidekick was shadowing him. The two of them saw us and immediately veered our way.

"Mr. Anderson," Detective Martins began, "have you found anything?"

"We've had two hits so far," I said, which caused both detective and consultant to stiffen with surprise. "The first was back there a bit. The dogs stopped at a circular wire display of books. Don't ask me why, other than my most recent novel was on it."

"I remember seeing that," Greg mused, mostly to himself.

"And the second?" Detective Martins asked.

I pointed at Jack's table. "Right here. In fact, if I didn't know any better, I'd say the dogs have singled out that package for Jack, there. Again, don't ask me why."

Detective Martins approached the table and pointed at the package. "Are you this package's recipient?"

Jack nodded. "I am."

"Do you recognize the sender?"

"As you can see, Detective," Jack began, using a tone of voice which suggested he was lecturing a room full of amateurs, "there is no return address. As for the shipping label, well, it looks as though it came from this city."

"Would you mind if I opened it?" Detective Martins asked. I could tell from the way Martins was talking that he was on full alert. "In fact, I'd like to insist on it, if that's all right with you?"

Jack's eyes had widened the instant he noticed how serious Detective Martins was behaving. He nodded and hastily stepped away from the table. The detective then produced a tiny pen knife and made a move to slice through the packing tape.

"Umm, am I the only one who's worried?" Jillian asked, as she started backing away from the table.

Stepping in front of her, I ended up snapping my fingers a few times. "Detective? Jillian has a good point. Should you be opening that thing in here? What if it's a ... you know, something which goes boom?"

"The bomb squad is standing by outside," Greg announced. "Perhaps we should let them deal with this?"

Detective Martins paled and hastily refolded his knife. "Of course, you're right. What was I thinking? Just a moment. We'll deal with this."

A few minutes later, a crew of three people, pushing a heavy metal cart, arrived. They were decked out in the full padding that I've seen bomb experts use when investigating a potentially live bomb. Jack's package, and every other package on the table, was carefully placed into the metal bin and rolled away. Ten minutes later, we got the news.

"They took thermal scans of it," Detective Martins told us, as he listened to the bomb squad's report on the phone. "There's nothing special about it. In fact, it looks like a drink bottle of some sort."

"You have my utter blessing to do with it as you see fit," Jack assured the detective.

"That goes for any package addressed to me, too," I added.

As it happened, Jack's package *did* contain a bottle. On it was a label I recognized. Irn Bru. It was touted as tasting like liquid bubble gum, and in case you were wondering about the name, well, it was pronounced *iron brew*. It was a bright orange liquid that was readily available in Scotland and various parts of the UK. Having been to Scotland myself, I can say that I've tried the local favorite, but apparently, it's an acquired taste.

Jack, apparently, had gone on record that this particular orange drink was one of his favorites when he visited the Highlands of Scotland during an international book tour. One fan must've paid attention, because they sent him a bottle. As for the other packages, that's all they were: gifts. And mine? Someone had sent me a claddagh pendant. For those who might not know, the claddagh is the internationally recognized symbol of Ireland. It has the appearance of two hands clasped around a heart, with a crown directly above the heart. Trust me, you'd recognize it if you saw it.

"How pretty!" Jillian said, once I showed the necklace to her. "You have very thoughtful fans."

My phone started ringing at the exact same time as Detective Martins'. We glanced at each other, shrugged, and took our respective calls.

"Zack?"

"Yeppers. Who's this?"

"It's Richard! What in the world have you been doing?"

"Excuse me? I've been helping the police. Why? What's going on?"

"Now they're saying you're trying to release some zombie drug? What in the world is going on over there? Are you trying to line us up for count-less lawsuits?"

"I've already spoken with the local police about this," I assured my rep. "They know I didn't say that. Well, I mean, I guess I did, but not in that order."

"Huh? Make sense, would you?"

"Richard, some teenage girl took everything I said during that live podcast I was on and spliced it together to make it sound like I'm some bio-terrorist. I'm not. Have you listened to it?"

"Yes, we have."

"Then, you'll be able to tell that it's not something I would say. I mean, all hail goddess Oya? I had never even heard of this damn Oya person until we started looking around."

"Well, that's true," Richard admitted. "I thought it sounded kinda funny."

"That's because the words were taken from different sentences. It's not going to flow well. It's a very amateurish move, if you ask me. Look, Richard, I need you to trust me. I'm going to get to the bottom of this. Detective Martins is headed back over. I'll keep you posted."

"Mr. Anderson," Detective Martins began, "I've been told we need to shut this convention down. The risk to the public is just too great. What if this girl has managed to get her hands on this devil's breath gunk? What if it's unleashed into the air here?"

"I wouldn't do that," Vance said, lowering his voice to a whisper.

"Would you like to run that by me again?" Detective Martins said, clearly surprised at Vance's reaction.

We all formed an impromptu huddle.

"Look," Vance was saying, "if you cancel this shindig now, then there's a strong likelihood that it'll go off early."

"How do you figure?" Gregory Plinth asked.

"You think our suspect has an accomplice," Martins scowled. "Of course. A backup, in case something happens to her, or else something happens to prematurely clear everyone out. We've got someone else to find, don't we?"

I nodded. "We do, indeed. And I think that's where these two will come in."

Martins checked his watch. "All right, here's the thing. We need to find this accomplice in the next fifteen minutes."

"What happens in fifteen minutes?" Jillian wanted to know.

Detective Martins made a sweeping gesture with his hand. "That's when this place officially opens. If we can't locate the accomplice by that time, and neutralize whatever threat there is, then the expo will have to be shut completely down."

"And that little snot wins," I grumbled. "This place will forever be known as the location of the book expo attack. Twice. Hey, do we have a rough estimate of how many people are due to arrive?"

"Nearly a thousand," Martins answered, using a grim tone. "Probably more. But, I can safely say that we have nearly forty officers here. They've begun their search."

I looked down at the dogs. "Well, let's see if we can make this easier for them. Sherlock? Watson? We've got an accomplice to find. Are you up for it?"

Sherlock rose to his feet and gave himself a thorough shaking. Watson was already standing. I felt the twin tugs on the leashes and couldn't help but smile. The dogs had already picked up on something. I could only hope that, in this case, it was a *someone*.

"Find 'em, guys," I heard Vance utter, from somewhere behind me.

"If anyone can do it, they can," Tori added.

We followed the dogs down several hallways, through a large meeting room currently filled with attendees, and then a second set of hallways. We made so many turns that I was hopelessly lost. Then again, I wasn't trying to find my way out. I had Jillian for that. What I wanted was to find whomever was helping Tina cause panic.

Hearing a number of footsteps coming from behind me, I noticed that not only did we have Martins and his consultant following our little group, but every time we passed a cop, that officer would inevitably circle around and start following us. It was like I was the Pied Piper, and everywhere I went, I was playing my flute. In less than ten minutes, we had, conservatively, at least thirty people following behind us.

"Don't let me down, guys," I pleaded, as I followed the dogs through yet another large conference room. This one was empty. "Do you guys know where you're going?"

We approached a single, closed door on the left side of the room. Both corgis turned to look at me, as if to say, *you may open the door, biped.*

"Oh, please, allow me, your Royal Canineships."

This drew a few snickers from somewhere behind me.

Surprisingly, we emerged into the same food court that we had been in before. I briefly wondered if a building this size had more than one place to grab a bite to eat, but I didn't have time to consider it. The dogs pulled me straight through the tables, which, thankfully, were devoid of people this time around. It also made it easier to spot who we were headed toward. There, sitting by herself at the table closest to the exit, was a blonde teenage girl. She had an identification card hanging from her neck, so I could only assume she had pretended to be a member of the staff, so as to gain early access back here. She turned to look at me and, the moment we locked eyes, I knew she was the one we were looking for. She let out a yelp of surprise and tried to push herself away from her table so she could make a run for it, only by the time she made it to her feet, the dogs were there.

Sherlock darted under her chair, while Watson circled around from the left. Now, bear in mind that Sherlock and Watson were still attached to their leashes. What happened? Well, the blonde girl's left foot became tied to her chair and her right became tied to the table itself. The moment she tried to run, everything crashed to the ground.

Detective Martins and nearly a dozen officers were there in a flash. One officer gently unclipped Sherlock from his tangled leash and held him out to me. Another untangled Watson and held her out to Vance, who quickly tucked the corgi close to his side.

"Well, well, what have we here?" Detective Martins asked. He noticed the bright pink backpack which had been dropped—and then kicked—under an adjacent table. He retrieved the bag and started to unzip it.

"You can't touch that bag!" the girl practically screamed. "I didn't give you permission!"

"This is an active crime scene," Detective Martins coolly returned. "It means I can. Mr. Anderson, do you recognize this girl by any chance?"

I stepped up to claim the recently disentangled leashes when I caught sight of the girl's face. Yes, I did know her. The last time I saw her, she and her three other friends were arguing among themselves outside this very building.

"I saw her with Tina," I said, nodding. "They're friends."

"She's no friend of mine," the girl shrieked.

Detective Martins started reaching for the bag, as though he was going to open it up. The four of us practically cried out *no* in unison. I, being closest, instantly swatted Martins' hand away from the pack.

"If there's any chance that bag contains what we suspect it does, are you sure you want to do that?"

The detective paled and immediately looked toward the door. As if he had been waiting for that exact moment, a guy in a hazmat suit appeared. He hurriedly took the bag outside, which caused us to follow, but from an extreme distance. We watched as the bag was unzipped, a hand reached inside, and then reappeared, holding … a handful of empty plastic bags.

"There are traces of a white powder visible inside each bag," the man in the hazmat suit reported.

With a look of sheer incredulity on his face, Detective Martins turned to the teenage girl and pointed at the bags.

"What is this? Where is the powder?"

The girl started sobbing.

We watched as the bags were dropped into a special canister, sealed, and carted away.

"What was in there?" Martins asked again. "So help me, if you don't want to see the inside of a jail cell for the next twenty years, you'll tell me!"

"I am so sorry! I never sh-should have agreed to th-this!"

"What did Tina want you to do?" Vance gently asked. "What was in there? Powdered sugar?"

"It was supposed to be a prank!" the teenager insisted. "I never thought Tina would take this so seriously!"

The girl broke down into hysterics. Great wracking sobs and wails were the only things that could be heard. I saw that Martins was ready to blow a gasket, so to speak, so I decided to see if we could possibly help out.

"Martins! Look, pal. These bags? They all held some type of powder, right?"

Detective Martins nodded. His angry red face began to revert to a healthy pink color.

"Listen, whatever this device is, it obviously hasn't gone off yet, right?"

Martins checked his watch. "We have less than five minutes."

"Then, let's make 'em count. If you had a large quantity of powder, and you wanted to infect as many people as possible, where would you put it?"

Vance nodded. "The ventilation system!"

"Look around, Detective Samuelson," Martins sighed. "This place is too big. There's no way we can search all of the ductwork in time."

I pointed at the corgis. "We found her; we can find this device. Have your bomb squad ready."

Martins' grim face nodded. "They will be. Should we evacuate?"

"Tina is already in custody, right?" Vance asked. Martins nodded.

Vance then pointed at the girl. "That means the only way to set it off, if it isn't already programmed to do so, would be by cell phone. Confiscate hers, would you?"

Martins nodded. "Gladly."

I looked at Sherlock and Watson. "Guys? You've been absolutely fantastic so far, but I really need you to come through for me. Somewhere out there is a large quantity of powder, and it's probably attached to some type of electronic device. We need to find it."

The dogs took off like a shot. Deciding we

needed to find this thing as quickly as possible, I let the dogs sprint ahead, which of course meant I had to sprint alongside them. Glancing back, I could see Vance, Detective Martins, and Gregory Plinth keeping up with me.

Sherlock and Watson led us to the opposite side of the food court and promptly ran through the closest open door. Running pell-mell down the hallway we were in, it felt as though the dogs were changing directions as abruptly as the light cycles from Disney's Tron movie. Once again, I could only hope that someone else knew how to backtrack out of here and return us to the food court.

The dogs skidded to a stop in front of a closed door. Looking up, I could see that it was a woman's restroom. Also of note was that we were now apparently in a seldom-used area of the convention center. Aside from my own labored breathing, and that of my companions, I couldn't hear or see anyone else. I looked at the door and then back at Detective Martins.

"Well?"

"Well, what? Go in, of course."

I knocked on the door and propped it open with my foot. "Hello? Anyone in here?"

There was no answer.

"I'm coming in, ladies. Make sure you're covered."

"There's no one in there, you goof," Vance quietly said, from directly behind me.

Once we were inside, the dogs headed for the

sinks, and then promptly went under them. Squatting, I could see that there was an air intake vent just a few inches above the floor. I looked back at Martins and then pointed at the vent.

"Oh, please let this be it," I heard Martins say.

The New Orleans detective fumbled with something on his belt, which I later saw was a multi-tool similar to the one I typically wear on my belt, and quickly removed the vent cover.

"Anything?" Vance hopefully asked.

"Plinth? You there?"

Gregory knelt down on the floor so he could peer under the sinks. "I'm here. What is it? Did you find something?"

"Call the bomb squad. Those dogs did it! We found it!"

EPILOGUE

W hat are these things called again?" Vance asked, as he cut off a corner of the dessert in front of him and popped it in his mouth. "Beignets? All right, I'll admit it. I like them."

"What's not to like?" Tori challenged. "They're a French pastry, consisting of a sweetened dough made using yeast, given square cuts, and dusted with powdered sugar."

"I don't think I'll look at powdered sugar the same way ever again," I chuckled.

"Seen too much of it lately, have you?" Vance teased.

"I'm just glad there was no way that nutjob girl could've gotten her hands on that devil's breath crap," I said, breathing a sigh of relief. "That was the best news ever, wasn't it? That there was nothing in those bags but powdered sugar? Made my day. Made my week, if you want to get technical."

It was now Tuesday, the following morning.

The four of us, including the two dogs, were sitting at a table at Café Beignet's outside patio. We had several hours to kill before we needed to be at the airport so we could head home.

"And here I thought writers led boring lives," Vance commented, as he popped the remaining piece of beignet in his mouth. "Hmmdve thaw herr 'eee eggsitmnn?"

Tori made the mistake of thumping her husband in the gut for speaking with his mouth full. However, since his mouth *was* full, and she just socked him in the stomach, it meant a white cloud of sugar whooshed out of his mouth, along with little pea-sized bits of half-chewed dough.

"Oh, ewww! That's gross!" Tori exclaimed.

I was laughing so hard I couldn't see straight. I held up a hand. "Did anyone else see that coming?"

Jillian had scooted her chair close to mine, so was therefore out of the danger zone. Tori, on the other hand, was now wearing a fine covering of sugar. She quickly excused herself to run to the bathroom so she could get cleaned up.

"I'm gonna get it for that one," Vance laughed. "Oh, well. Chalk it up as another memory we won't ever forget. Hey, Zack, listen. Before Tori gets back, I just wanted to tell you thanks for doing this for us. I owe you big."

"Don't sweat it, pal," I assured him. "It's what friends do. Besides, I'd say all of us are benefitting, wouldn't you think? I mean, hey, we have an open ticket to fly to London—all expenses paid—whenever we want. We just have to let MCU know so they can set up some type of event."

"There will be no complaints coming from me," Vance promised.

"Have you heard from Chief Nelson yet?" I asked.

Vance nodded and grinned. "He's honoring the bet. Since the dogs solved the case before the local boys, which made PV look amazingly good these last couple of days, I can now say I'm senior detective."

"Congrats, pal. You earned it. What? What's the matter?"

"You do realize what I have to do now, don't you?"

"Hmm? What's that?"

"I should make you shave your head, too."

"Your performance of that song!" I chuckled. "I had completely forgotten about it."

"Yeah, well, I haven't. Isn't there enough incriminating evidence about me on YouTube? I don't need anything else, thank you very much."

"Aww, come on! You obviously made Chief Nelson's day!"

"At what price?" Vance groaned.

"Well, you're a good sport," I decided. "I'm just thankful I get to be there."

Vance shook his head. "Nope. I'm doing this by myself. Tori will be the one recording this disaster. No one else is allowed near me."

"Except me," I proudly proclaimed. "Chief Nelson gave me the role of videographer."

Vance groaned and rolled his eyes. "Oh, that's just great. You could've turned him down, you know."

Tori was back five minutes later. She gave Vance an unreadable look as she slid into her chair. After a few moments, she was looking my way.

"Did that detective fellow ever say anything about the device you guys found in the ladies' bathroom?"

I nodded. "Yeah, a little bit. It was of a very basic design. It had a cell phone trigger, and it was connected to a mini fan. That's the funny part. Had it actually gone off, it probably wouldn't have done a darn thing. The fan wasn't strong enough to move that much powder anywhere. On top of which, it was nice outside, so the building's heating and cooling systems were off."

I snorted with amusement. "Talk about some poor planning."

"She was just a girl," Jillian reminded me. "I wonder what her motive was? Yes, I know she preferred going to her comic book conventions, but there had to be more to it than that."

Vance pulled out his notebook from an inner pocket. "I can help there. A little, anyway. Let's see. Christina Marie Vallot, sixteen. Lives with her father, no mother. Die-hard comic book fan. Loves superheroes, and dressing up as her favorite characters. Works in her dad's restaurant. No social life. Looks like going to these comic book conventions was the only thing she did for fun. Take that away from her and what do you get?"

"That poor girl. So much rage for one so young," Jillian lamented.

"That *poor girl* is responsible for killing a man," Tori reminded her.

"What was the story with that?" I asked, as I turned to Vance.

"I asked about that, too," Vance said. He flipped a few pages in his notebook. "The answer lies with the victim, and what he had been holding. The security team went back through the CCTV footage and saw that his death was just a freak accident."

"What had he been holding?" I asked.

Vance consulted his notes. "Hang on, I wrote it down. There it is. It's called a dragon-claw crescent knife. I guess it was used in some movie or television series. Anyway, on the handle part, there were several long spikes. When everyone panicked and fought like crazy to leave the convention center, this guy was holding his knife, but ended up slipping and falling to the floor. Panicked people are a dangerous group. No one helped the guy up. In fact, several people stepped on him, and that's how we're figuring he ended up with two puncture marks on his chest. He was killed with his own weapon."

"What happened to the weapon?" Jillian asked.

"Someone else picked it up and absconded with it," Vance said.

"I hope that someone gets arrested," I said,

frowning. "That's thievery, no matter how you look at it."

"I'd like to know something," Jillian announced. She looked at Vance and gave him a smile. "What was the link to voodoo? Did Tina ever say?"

Vance looked at me and shrugged. "Sorry. I don't know about that."

"I asked that same question of Gregory," I said. "I can tell you what he told me." Heads were nodding. Clearing my throat, I attempted my best Tim Curry impersonation. "Voodoo was just a red herring."

Vance snotted his soda. Tori snorted with surprise while Jillian stared at me, open-mouthed. A few moments later, she began giggling.

"Voodoo is a red herring? Seriously? I can't believe you just said that."

"Red herring?" Vance repeated, as he wiped his nose with the napkin Tori handed him. "No one talks like that anymore. Not since …"

"*Clue*, the movie?" I said, offering Vance a lopsided smile.

Vance snapped his fingers. "Yeah! That's where I heard it. What's the line? Communism was a red herring? What made you think of that just now?"

"We watched it in our room last night," I confessed. "Love that movie."

"Dork," Vance laughed. "So, before we sign off on this adventure, are we all agreed? Video of *them* goes up on YouTube?"

"Just make sure you add the appropriate hashtags," Jillian said. "That way, everyone will know who is competing and where they work."

"You're a master of social media, too?" I asked, as I turned to Jillian. Wrapping my arm around her shoulders, we turned to look at the next table over. "How are our pals doing? Hey, Martins? Mr. Plinth? Having any trouble?"

Two humungous bowls of half-eaten ice cream were in front of the men. Each, I might add, looked as though they were going to barf should they eat another bite. Martins looked my way and gave me a feeble thumbs-up. Laughing, we turned back to our own table and began to gather everything together so it could be thrown away. As I dumped the first load into the trash receptacle, I heard Jillian's phone chime, announcing the arrival of a text message. That's when I heard her gasp.

Dropping the tray onto the stack of empties, I turned to see my fiancée clutching her phone so hard that her knuckles were turning white. Tori and Vance made it to her first and quickly guided her into the closest chair.

"What is it?" I asked, growing alarmed. "What's wrong?"

Jillian held up her phone. "It's from Joshua. Oh, Zachary, he's in trouble!"

Taking the phone from her trembling hands, I read for myself the message my future brother-in-law had sent.

OUT OF TIME. HEADNG UNDER. REMBR CHST.

"What does it mean?" I cautiously asked.

"It's code," Jillian sobbed. "Out of time must mean he's being pursued. Heading under? He's going into hiding."

"And that last bit?" Vance gently asked. "What does that mean?"

"Remember, what?" I wondered aloud. "Remember Christ? Chest? The silver chest from Ireland?"

"Zachary, we have to help him!"

"Isn't he in the military?" I asked. "Why would he even need our help?"

"Haven't I told you?" Jillian said, between tears. "Joshua has been on loan to MI6 for the last couple of years!"

AUTHOR'S NOTE

There, that wasn't too bad, was it? I mean, I don't like dropping cliffhangers, but this one was pretty close. Besides, I've been asked over and over when I was going to get the dogs over to England, to be thanked by the queen, of course, and I thought, why not? I saw a story brewing, so I'm glad I'm finally able to get it started. Zack will finally get to meet Jillian's long-absent brother, Joshua!

I hope you enjoyed reading about New Orleans. If you ever have a chance to make it out there, trust me, it's worth seeing. Many of the descriptions don't do the city justice. Those shops along Bourbon Street? Walking through the French Quarter? It must be experienced to be truly appreciated.

So, up next we have Case of the Missing Marine. We get to find out why Joshua sent the silver chest to Zack in the first place. We get to learn about his involvement in MI6, and yes, Sherlock and Watson will be able to meet the queen. With this one story, I get to tie up several loose ends, so I hope you plan on sticking with me for the next adventure!

I will be releasing my latest fantasy story by the end of summer. If you enjoy reading about dragons, and like light-hearted adventure stories, I would encourage you to give it a try. I've had a lot of fun with it.

That's it for now. Summer is in full swing here, and as I look at the outside temperature, it is a sweltering 113°F. Ugh. I hope it's cooler where you are!

Happy reading!

J.
June, 2021

Thank you so much for taking the time to read *Case of the Ragin' Cajun*. If you enjoyed the story, please consider leaving a review wherever you purchased the book. Authors love reviews, and the more reviews they can get, the easier they can be found at the large online retailers.

Until next time!

J.

Zack and the dogs will return, in *Case of the Missing Marine* (Corgi Case Files #14) - Fall, 2021

Sherlock and Watson have been invited to Buckingham Palace, for a meeting with the queen herself. So, Zack, Jillian, and the dogs head across the Atlantic. There, Jillian is shocked to learn her US Marine brother has been working with MI6, and is currently missing. They soon discover Joshua was working on a top secret project, and nearly every foreign government wants to get their hands on him.

Can Zack and the dogs figure out what Joshua has been working on? Will they be able to find him before someone else does? Will Zack be able to wrap this up in time so that he doesn't miss his own wedding?

THE CORGI CASE FILES SERIES
Available in e-book and paperback

Case of the One-Eyed Tiger
Case of the Fleet-Footed Mummy
Case of the Holiday Hijinks
Case of the Pilfered Pooches
Case of the Muffin Murders
Case of the Chatty Roadrunner
Case of the Highland House Haunting
Case of the Ostentatious Otters
Case of the Dysfunctional Daredevils
Case of the Abandoned Bones
Case of the Great Cranberry Caper
Case of the Shady Shamrock
Case of the Ragin' Cajun
Case of the Missing Marine (available now for pre-order)

If you enjoy Epic Fantasy, check out Jeff's other series:
Pirates of Perz
Tales of Lentari
Bakkian Chronicles

Made in the USA
Coppell, TX
10 August 2023

20197592R00164